TO BE THE BEST
Book Three: Overtime

By H. L. Hertel

HH Castle-Mac Publishing
St Louis Park, MN

Books By H. L. HERTEL

TO BE THE BEST: SIX MINUTES

TO BE THE BEST: REMATCH

TO BE THE BEST: OVERTIME

Copyright © 2016 H. L. Hertel

To Be The Best: Overtime is a work of fiction. Names, places and incidents either are products of the author's imagination or are used fictitiously.

ISBN: 978-0-9826684-1-2

Published by HH Castle-Mac Publishing, St Louis Park, MN

Dedication

This book is dedicated to my daughter, Lillian. She is my pride and joy and "the best" at so many things. I am constantly amazed as I watch her grow and see just how remarkable a human can be.

Acknowledgements

Each time I finish a book, I look back in amazement at how it all came together. This book may have been more difficult to write than the first two simply because there was no backing out of it after I announced in a radio interview for *Rematch* that the skeleton for the third book was already complete. Given the integrity theme in *Rematch,* I had to follow through with same level of commitment to complete *Overtime.*

Yet, writer's block is a painful thing and, had it not been for all of the fans of the first two books hounding me at book signings, wrestling tournaments and over the internet, it would have been much easier to simply call it good after two.

I'm humbled by the *To Be The Best* fans who came back for thirds and am grateful for the undying support of my usual cast of characters. My wife Lisa is always the first one to get the finished manuscript and finds edits and story-line discrepancies that would otherwise go unquestioned.

Heidi, Brian and T once again scoured the final product and pointed out items that casual wrestling fans would miss but would frustrate die-hard ones. Then Bill came through again with final edits and plot questions which only someone with decades of experience in writing and editing would notice.

Finally, the cover models for this book came through as I am blessed to have state-placers and All-Americans filling up the awards stand so that Amy could work her graphical magic.

Thank you all for your roles in making this book solid and making it a reality!

Introduction

At some point, someone is bound to ask me, "Why did it take so long to write your third book?" so I may as well address this up front and note that this is the quickest I've ever written a book.

The original *To Be The Best* took 14 years from the time the original first chapter was written until the time it was published. *Rematch* was published three years later but, in truth, was largely written in tandem with the original. *Overtime*, on the other hand was originally just going to be a paragraph in the *Rematch* Epilogue until I was rocked by an "aha" moment on my way to work one day when *Rematch* was going through final editing.

The books are largely written around Nick's growth as a wrestler and a human being. His declarations in the first book of, "I'm not going to lose this match!" and in the second of, "I'm not saying that I CAN'T wrestle, I'm saying I WON'T!" tell us of his commitment and what he sees as important in life. On that fateful drive to work in 2011, I realized that the key to propelling him into the rest of his life would stem from events that would lead him to tell his coach, "I remember that I wanted to die."

Since much of my writing happens in the middle of the night (after the 50+ hour work week and family activities), or on those rare weekends during which my family goes somewhere (Girl Scout camp) and leaves me home alone, it takes a while to get to a final product. The side-projects never seem to end as I was also asked to write the *To Be The Best Prequel* for a wrestling magazine in 2013, and convert the original book into a stage play but, eventually the story all comes together and we review what we have and conclude, "That is the one. That is how the series should end."

Thank you for your patience and support. Enjoy the final leg of the journey.

Prologue

Nick Castle watched the ceiling getting further away and braced himself for the imminent impact with the mat.

Chester Troftgruben's sweat-soaked practice shirt read, "Watch Them Fly" and had a picture of two wrestlers on it in very much the same positions he and Nick were currently in – Nick, unfortunately, resembled the wrestler being thrown – frozen in mid-air, feet facing the lights.

Thud.

Upon hitting the mat, Nick immediately rolled to his belly before Chester could earn any back points. Defensive positioning and countering had been the focus of the prior two days of wrestling camp. The lessons had resonated well with Nick, although apparently not well enough to have full effect versus the likes of Chester.

Oddly, the two boys had become fairly close friends over the course of the summer. Having only wrestled each other in one regular season match during their two illustrious careers, a junior-year pre-Christmas Tournament semi-final match which saw Chester give Nick a sound thrashing, the two had no reason to build up any animosity. Further, they soon found significant common ground as each had finished his respective junior year ranked high going into the state tournament (Nick first at 140 pounds and Chester second at 152 pounds) but failed to bring home state gold. This left unfinished business for both as fall approached.

Nick both relished and despised being matched with Chester as his practice partner. Although he had added nearly ten pounds of muscle since February, Nick still looked scrawny and awkward versus the broader, stronger Troftgruben who himself had been lifting and now weighed close to 170 pounds. This was the second and final summer camp the two had attended in their home state and, given the dearth of similarly-sized wrestlers who could give Chester any kind of competition, Nick had become the default opponent assigned to Chester by the camp coaches. This pushed Nick to his limits and made him better while at the same time bruising both the smaller boy's body and ego.

The two had also crossed paths at a pair of out-of-state camps and had roomed together at both the second camp and at Junior Nationals. Nick's older brother Ron referred to Chester as "The Cheater" since he had been held back in eighth grade for no apparent reason. He certainly seemed bright enough to Nick, which partially confirmed Ron's conjecture that Chester had intentionally failed in order to notch an additional year of physical and emotional maturity versus his wrestling opponents. With Chester's birthday in early November and Nick's in late July, it created a gap of nearly two years.

All of this aside, Nick enjoyed his practice partner's company when they weren't on the mat. He looked forward to crossing paths at several tournaments during the season as their weight difference would certainly keep them from going head-to-head.

As Nick worked to stand up and gain hand control, he pitied the wrestlers who would face either him or Chester this season. The two had both been so diligent and focused on their goals of winning the state championship that others would be best served to stay out of their way.

Chapter 1

The vehicle made its way slowly down the interstate. Blizzard conditions were keeping most drivers off of the road ... but most drivers did not need to reach their destination this badly.

The car's appearance was as pristine as its driver was tarnished, his body tense as he leaned forward, hoping that it would help him see through the snow.

Five years. Had it really been that long? In some ways, it felt like a lifetime since he had more-or-less been run out of town. Over that time, he had had many reasons for making the trip back. Heck, his in-laws lived just over an hour away. Yet, he had always found an excuse to not come back to the place which held so many good memories entangled with and strangled by just as many bad ones.

He let himself grin as he saw the sign for the second exit. It had taken nearly fifteen minutes to get from the first city limits sign three miles back to this exit he needed. Conditions were getting worse as he engaged his blinker and headed for the exit ramp, the one that would send him through downtown and bring him to his final destination.

He turned on the radio, happy to finally get a signal and fumbled with the dial until he found something reasonable. Don Henley's New York Minute had never ranked among his favorites but it seemed strangely symbolic of his plight. He let it play.

It took another fifteen minutes of white knuckle driving before he was able to cross the bridge. It was fortunate for the man that the car had the muscle he lacked these days, propelling him through the drifts in the half-plowed streets and eventually bringing him to a parking spot in the Whitey's Wonderbar lot.

He said a quick prayer before leaving the car. This was his final hope. It had to work out.

Donning his gloves and pulling a hat over his bald head, he nearly collided with an inebriated man, making his way through the lot.

"Sweet ride," the drunk man commented. "1965 Mustang."

" '66," Sean MacCallister *corrected him with a small smile, and continued his journey into the bar.*

* * *

The inside of the bar had not changed much over time. It still reeked of cigarette smoke, stale beer and plenty of other unpleasant odors.

Sean went straight to the bar, knowing that what he sought was not on the menu. There weren't many patrons out on such a miserable night. There were a few tables of college kids who now seemed awfully young to him. Across the bar was a long-haired, hippie-looking kid in major need of a shave. His stringy hair and beard were unkempt while his bleary eyes were tell-tale signs that he was well beyond the legal limit. Other than an old couple that was getting ready to leave, nobody else was in the bar.

"What will you have?" the bartender asked.

All Sean really wanted was a water and some information but he felt sheepish about not ordering. He was down to his last $50 and his credit card was maxed out so he would have to find ways to economically make something work.

"Can I get your appetizer menu?" he asked. "Also, is Kelly Veers working tonight?"

The bartender stopped.

"Veers? He quit six months ago."

Sean's heart sank ... after making all of that effort, driving a hundred miles through snow and cold and all to end up sitting in a dank bar by himself. He closed his eyes and inhaled deeply. After his recent months of pain and anguish, he really would have welcomed something, anything, going right tonight ... perhaps he had just been made to suffer.

When the bartender came back with a menu, Sean looked up and noticed that the hairy guy across the bar was staring at him. It made him uncomfortable but, when the man nodded at him, he nodded back to be polite.

Sean began looking at the menu but could see in his peripheral vision that the hippie was getting up from his seat and staggering around the bar toward him.

"Please let him be heading to the bathroom," MacCallister hoped. The last thing Sean needed was to be hit up for money or to find other trouble.

Out of the corner of his eye, Sean could see the man get to the corner of the bar and stop. He was getting an uneasy feeling that the man would soon make his way over and talk to him.

"Drunk," Sean thought, trying to focus on the menu and ignore the man. "Just come over and hit me up for a drink or some spare change and be done with it."

For a moment, he became self-righteous, not able to recall a time in the days that he was drinking and constantly broke that he had ever begged strangers for alcohol. With all of the progress he had made recovering in some areas of his life, he figured that his seemingly unending monetary woes would have to improve eventually.

"Tostacos are only a buck?" MacCallister asked the bartender, hoping that the conversation would encourage the hairy man to move on.

"Only after 10:00," the bartender replied.

Sean fumed a bit as he sensed the man to his left take a step closer.

"Do you have a problem?!" Sean didn't vocalize the question yet but promised himself that he would if the man approached further. Sensing more movement, he took a deep breath and turned to let the man have it.

"Coach?"

The word and the voice speaking it created a sudden surge of emotion. Sean reeled to look at the man and got a bit misty at the face he saw.

"Nick?"

"I thought that was you, Coach. I almost didn't recognize you without your hair."

Sean stood and, two steps later, gave his stoic former protégé a big bear hug, trying not to let the younger man see him tear up.

"It looks like you're making up for all of the hair I shaved off," Sean replied.

"Yeah," Nick smirked, slurring his words a bit. "I decided to grow a finals beard at the end of spring semester."

"You know you're supposed to shave that when finals are over," Sean remarked.

"It was more efficient to just leave it so I wouldn't have to grow a fresh one this semester," Nick joked.

The two stood and looked at each other for another few moments.

"Do you have time to catch up a bit?" Sean finally asked, knowing that he himself had no real place to go.

"My girlfriend was supposed to pick me up but, judging by the argument we had last night and the fact that she was supposed to *be here two hours ago, I'm guessing that I may have all the time in the world."*

The two found a booth and ordered some appetizers. Nick switched to drinking water while Sean ordered a hot tea to help remove the chill.

"I can't believe you're old enough to be in here," Sean commented. "Last time I saw you, you were in high school."

"... and now I'm 21," Nick interrupted. "A lot has happened since you coached Ron and me at Riverside my junior year."

Sean thought about how solid Nick had been that year and wondered what had happened. Nick had been ranked first in state going into the state tournament that year and still had another season to go. Surely he must have gotten some interest from college programs.

"Well, why don't you fill me in on the details of your senior season?" Sean requested, and immediately kicked himself as Nick's face got solemn. Sean bit his lip, remembering the one thing he knew for sure – how the state tournament had ended awkwardly.

Yet Nick seemed to want to talk.

"Well," the younger man began, "my senior season was literally just a continuation of my junior year. I went straight from the high school season as a junior into spring Freestyle and Greco, into summer camps and tournaments, and then ran cross country and lifted weights all fall to get ready. I was convinced that I was unstoppable and everything started perfectly until life proved otherwise ..."

Chapter 2

Nick entered the Riverside wrestling room and looked around. He knew he wasn't supposed to be there but surely it was fine given the circumstances.

There was his brother's name, carved into the Ring of Honor, commemorated alongside Grunseth, Palmer, Welsh and so many others. More importantly to Nick on this day was that a mason was there, carving the next name into the brick wall.

Nick was downright giddy. How many years had he waited for this day? How many thousands of hours had he spent practicing, preparing and competing to win a state title. And now, it would be the icing on the cake, a state title and a place in the Ring of Honor to cement his place in history. He stood and watched the mason as the "N" started to take shape in the bricks. The boy closed his eyes and breathed deeply, completely at peace with the world.

"Nick, you've got to go."

Busted! The peace turned to fear as the odd-looking man in the suit walked toward him.

"You don't belong here. Let's go," the man repeated.

"But ..." Nick motioned toward the mason but the man was gone, Nick's name was gone ... the wall was completely untouched.

The dread filled and overwhelmed him like a flash flood, appearing out of nowhere and sweeping him away with hopelessness. He had not won the state title and he didn't belong on Kreitzer's Riverside team. He began to shudder and couldn't speak or move.

"Nick?"

The boy awoke to his father's voice.

"Nick, we've got to go if you're going to ride into town with me."

The man paused and looked at his shaken son.

"Are you ok?"

Nick's heart was beating fast as he tried to remind himself that it was a dream. It was a recurring nightmare that had haunted him a dozen times since the end of his junior year but it was only a dream.

The boy opened his dry mouth and nodded, looking to the man while leaving his warm covers for the chilly morning air, uncertain as to whether the goose bumps were from the nightmare or the brisk air.

"Power through it, Nick!" the boy thought. "You chose not to wrestle at state last year. It was the right choice, even if it didn't help Coach MacCallister. That is behind you now. Focus on this year."

This morning's workout would get him one step closer to his dream of winning a state wrestling championship and to making the nightmare disappear for good.

Chapter 3

He was running again. The early morning workout routine had become so much a part of his life that he could no longer imagine not running. What would happen when he fulfilled his dream of becoming a state champion? Would he continue to strive in the same way?

He pondered the question for a moment. There were certainly plenty of doubters who would tell him to not worry – he wasn't going to be the champ – he would always only be "the young one."

He had heard it again at a pre-season tournament a month earlier. It had taken all of his self-control, and some steering from his dad, to keep from getting in the face of the old man in the front row, jabbering loudly to his friend.

"That's the young one. He'll never be like the old one – the legend. He had a nice season last year but he didn't get the state title ... probably never will. The old one had grit and made everything look easy. For the young one, he's shown he can win, but it's never pretty."

Up the stairs and down the hall, chased by his demons he focused on escaping from the shadows – escaping from being the "wanna be" wrestler in the family.

The school opened its doors at 6:00 a.m. so he arrived at 5:58, waiting in the cold until he saw Austin, the custodian. The friendly old man always smiled at him, but this morning Austin had made the mistake of bringing up the forbidden subject.

"Wrestling starts tomorrow," the old man had commented, receiving a friendly nod in response from the boy.

"I hear that new boy is something else. People are saying that he's going to bring us a state title this year. Are you excited about that?"

It was all the boy could do to keep his anger under control and push out a positive-sounding grunt under his breath. As if it wasn't bad enough that he was living in the family shadow, now he would also have to fight from under the weight of the reputation of this new teammate – Nick Castle.

He unwillingly said the boy's name and then spat the taste of it from his mouth.

Last year, Tanner had taken Castle down and put him straight to his back. He had gotten within an instant of pinning the upperclassman before the boy had wiggled free and come back to win.

He sprinted down the hall, thinking of that match. Castle had been ranked number one in the state. Tanner had been a freshman, looking to improve his seeding going into the conference tournament. His dad had gotten after him for not pinning Castle when he had the chance. Now, Tanner Nestor's dad and coach was welcoming Castle with open arms to the South wrestling program. It made him sick to welcome the enemy into the fold.

Why did Castle have to move now? Why couldn't his family just stay where they were, far away from the South school district? Let him keep wrestling for Riverside. Let Tanner have the 152 varsity spot.

"He's not that great," Tanner thought. "He wins matches but he doesn't even look like a wrestler. That's probably why no universities have recruited him."

Tanner raced down the final set of stairs and found himself just in front of the wrestling room, intentionally ignoring the plaque with plates housing the names of the few state title winners from South's non-storied wrestling history. Tanner Nestor's last name was on that plaque three times ... his first name, not at all. Twenty years earlier, Tanner's dad had won as a freshman, a junior and a senior. In the subsequent years, so few wrestlers had won titles that the school had chosen to also include on the plaque several wrestlers who had come close. Coach Nestor was the lone superstar.

"Dad may be the legend today," Tanner thought. "And Castle might be the latest school hero ..."

Tanner stood for a moment and resisted one final urge to examine the plaque to ensure that they hadn't placed Castle's name on it in advance. He then stubbornly headed for the showers with a chip on his shoulder.

"... but the new season starts tomorrow. I'm going to blow all of them away."

Chapter 4

There was a buzzing somewhere in the background – a long, sustained hum that didn't seem to have a purpose, yet had no intention of tapering down. Eventually, it droned on long enough to create a spark in Sean's exhausted mind.

"There is something flat and solid under my head," was the first thought that drifted into the young man's brain. After months of solving business problems, small and large, he was about to piece together where he had fallen asleep without opening his eyes.

The garage floor and his home office desk were the two most likely suspects. His car project made him smile but, given that the surface under his head and hands was far too warm and smooth to be cement, he was inclined to believe it was the latter. Besides, there was a cushion of some sort under his butt which told him that, when he crashed, he was sitting in a chair.

"Ok, so I'm at my desk," he thought, slowly drifting into the next phase of consciousness. He opened one eye a crack and peered at the lamp and stack of papers that first entered his line of vision.

"Ugh," he thought, realizing that he had not made it home.

It was worse than he had initially thought. Not only had he failed to make it to his bed, he hadn't even left work.

He squinted, trying to get a good look at his desk clock.

"3:27." In two and a half hours, he would complete a twenty-four hour cycle at work.

How long had he been asleep? He vaguely remembered 11:00. That was when he had gone for another cup of coffee which he now noticed was sitting, untouched, two feet from his head.

The blood was flowing faster now, waking him up, and reminding him of his night's plight. Jeremy had called in sick, again, and the timing couldn't have been worse. Then again, not much had been easy the past three months.

Sean had gotten off to a strong start at his new job the previous February. He had immediately gone to work building relationships and learning the technology. Into May, he had offset his cognitive problems by throwing extra hours into his work ... early mornings, late nights and every weekend. His company and work had been his sole focus.

Then came his miracle and his angel. The experimental surgery to repair his damaged brain had gone well. Sean's clarity had improved and he had not experienced a migraine post-surgery. Even better, Julee had finished her degree and accepted a teaching job just two hours away. The two officially became a couple over the summer as Sean had added his final college coursework to his overflowing plate, graduating in August thanks again to excruciatingly long hours and weekends without reprieve. All of this had added to his credibility and made him a huge success at work. He earned his first promotion that same month.

Then started the dark times. The company was acquired by a larger corporation and the fallout began immediately. Larry Darkins, the general manager who brought Sean on board and served as his mentor was dismissed the first day, before he could even return from his vacation. Project timelines were condensed to force new products through by the end of the year in an effort to show immediate value to the new parent company. Sean's exhausted engineering friends took solace only from the fact that they remained employed while several other groups of engineers had been laid off upon announcement of the acquisition.

Sean's "Project Roadrunner" seemed to take on a new meaning as it seemed that all Sean and the team were doing was running to meet deadline after deadline.

Sean had been given a direct report named Jeremy to help him with a project audit and the ever-increasing volume of reports and updates needed by the new parent company and its board. In some ways, Jeremy had been more of a hindrance than a help. He was four years older than Sean but had initially failed as an engineer, relying on political astuteness to find a new role with the old regime and somehow hang on through the first two waves of lay-offs under new management.

Sean liked Jeremy as the man went out of his way to be vibrant and agreeable around Sean. It was unfortunate that Jeremy lacked the basic necessity of his role – attention to detail. This resulted in Sean having to review every document three to four times to ensure that nothing was incorrectly communicated to company management or the government auditors who seemed to always be around.

Jeremy also lacked reliability. In prior years, when Sean was still irresponsibly drinking, he had often gone to work and to class still feeling the effects of his prior night's binge. However, he had never actually missed work because of it and couldn't understand how anyone could be selfish enough to skip work when they knew that others on their team would have to work through the night to meet the already-tight deadlines. This would definitely show up on Jeremy's performance review.

Sean reached for his coffee and took a sip of the lukewarm beverage. He still had a few hours of reports to prepare and review, thus there would be no time to take the train home for a shower and change of clothes and make it back in time. He would look wrinkled and disheveled but he would find a way to meet this morning's deadline.

Chapter 5

Nick felt warm and secure as he held Sandi close. He thought about how perfect life was at that moment and how so much of what he wanted in life, he already held in his arms.

He watched the girl's face as the movie ended with the medallion ceremony at the rebel base. The heroes turned to be recognized, the assembly applauded, the wookie howled and the credits rolled.

After watching so many artsy movies with her, it was finally been time for her to watch *Star Wars* with him. By the look on her face, she seemed reasonably satisfied.

She turned her face toward him and he kissed her on the cheek.

"Well?" he asked.

"It was good," she said, a bit tentatively.

Whether her positive report reflected true enjoyment of the movie or a valiant effort to save his feelings didn't matter. Either reason was an additional one to love her.

"But ..." she started.

Nick tensed.

"... I don't get the ending."

"Which part?" Being an authority on all things *Star Wars*, surely he could add clarity.

"Luke Skywalker and Han Solo got medals, but why not Chewbacca?"

Nick smiled and kissed her again.

"Do you know how many times I've asked that same question?" the boy replied. "Chewie played at least as big a role as Han did. In fact, according to the *Star Wars* radio drama, it is Chewie that convinced Han to come back to save Luke in the first place."

She leaned in and kissed him on the lips.

"It's sad that all of his hard work didn't earn him a medal," Sandi stated, turning back to face the TV and pushing her shoulder blades snug against the boy. He responded by hugging her tight and kissing her blonde hair.

It was nice to spend some time holding her. In the near future, chances to do so would be severely limited. It was Monday evening and the first wrestling practice of the season would be Tuesday. As if this limit on Nick's free time wouldn't make things difficult enough, Sandi planned to try out for a show in early December which would consume her through early February at which time he would be completely inundated with activity in his push toward the state tournament. It wasn't quite as bad as the previous summer when she had spent two months in France, but it seemed like he would see her about as infrequently.

High school relationships are tough when time together is scarce. If Nick had been able to see Sandi in the halls at school, it would help. Unfortunately, that was no longer an option either. Nick's grandfather had passed away unexpectedly the prior spring causing Nick's father to take over the farm and move his family to the farmstead ten miles south of town. This put Nick in the South High School district while Sandi stayed at Riverside. Given Nick's unresolved issues with Assistant Principal Kreitzer from the year before, the boy was able to find a silver lining to the break.

Then came the call from Riverside's Principal Skinner. The man had made Nick extremely uncomfortable when he had encouraged the boy to petition to come back to Riverside.

"The kids on the north side of town don't have a lot of outstanding role models," the man had stated. "You are someone that a lot of elementary and junior high boys look up to. You get good grades, you typically stay out of trouble, and your hard work has led to wrestling success. Please consider staying and giving them hope."

It had almost made Nick change his mind. He had coached fifth and sixth grade intramural wrestling for two seasons, and during the past spring had spread himself thin, volunteering as a coach at two different north-end elementary schools. Sandi had found it extremely endearing when some of those tiny wrestlers had approached Nick at the mall. They were all proud to tell him about how they were continuing to wrestle and a few had friends in tow who asked for Nick's autograph.

"I'm going to win the state title and get my name on Riverside's wrestling wall, just like you," a messy-haired youth with buck teeth had told Nick that day.

Nick hadn't had the heart to tell them that he had already transferred schools and, like Dino, Nick had come so close but hadn't gotten his name on the wall.

"Dino, Chewbacca and me," Nick thought, "Coulda, woulda, and shoulda gotten the glory ... but it wasn't meant to be."

He hugged Sandi again, holding her close.

"Someday they'll set things right and Chewbacca will get his medal," he whispered in her ear.

In the meantime, Nick had his own medal to pursue.

Chapter 6

Sean walked slowly toward the copy room with mixed emotions. It was nearly 6:30 p.m. and, if things went well, he would be leaving work in less than half an hour.

No day that begins with waking up at your office desk can be perceived as "great" but he got his reports turned in on time and had heard second-hand that the business unit president was delighted with his project's progress. He lauded his engineers for their extra efforts and they left by 5:00 for happy hour to celebrate the victory.

It wasn't a big surprise that Jeremy had joined the engineers' team for their festivities. Even after calling in sick the previous day, the man somehow was feeling up for socializing 36 hours later.

"36 hours," Sean thought. "I've been at work for over 36 hours and have the body odor to prove it. Hopefully nobody else is around to notice."

The high point of the day had been a voicemail Julee left while he was in his morning meetings, "Hey MacCallister. I like you. I think you're nice."

It was simple and straightforward and raised his spirits. It was very cute, just like Julee herself. How did he deserve such a wonderful girlfriend who instinctively knew just when he needed a little extra cheering up?

The hallway was semi-dark after hours which would help to hide his wrinkled shirt and the excessive stubble which had grown far beyond a 5:00 shadow.

He entered the copy room and his jaw dropped. The words, "That is the most beautiful woman I've ever seen," shot through his mind instinctually. She looked like a supermodel, but somehow more attractive.

She stood talking with a man he recognized from accounting. Neither seemed to notice him initially which was fine by Sean, given his appearance. Besides, he wasn't in the copy room to socialize, he was there to make copies for the following morning's 8:00 meeting. The pilot customer for their new product was insisting on additional features, and Sean would need to lead the charge to show that their condensed timeline could in no way accommodate any scope creep.

Approaching the copier, he glanced at the woman out of the corner of his eye. She was wearing a navy blue suit coat and skirt and, as a learned reflex, he checked her left hand – no ring.

"What am I doing," he thought. "I've got a girlfriend. I'm not going to ruin that by chasing some other woman, regardless of how attractive she is."

He forced his attention back to the copy machine and took care of his business. Fifteen copies of twenty pages each – that shouldn't take too long. Yet, as the sheets of paper rolled through the machine, he found his gaze falling in her direction.

"Man! Look how hot she is. I bet she's totally full of herself," his tired mind processed.

To Sean's surprise and horror, the woman and her colleague looked in his direction as the first copy rolled out of the machine and was stapled.

"You're MacCallister, right?" the man called out.

"Yes," Sean answered with a sheepish smile, feeling a bit self-conscious about his disheveled appearance. As it was only the man who addressed him, he confirmed to himself that his suspicions about the woman's vanity were true ... for a moment.

"You're the Roadrunner Project Manager," she said.

"I am," he confirmed, unable to believe that she was striking up a conversation with him.

"I'm sorry," the man cut in. "I should have introduced you. Sean, this is Enid."

"Enid?" Sean thought. The only Enid he had ever known was his grouchy 80-year-old neighbor from his childhood who had nothing on this new Enid.

"Thank you, DuWayne," Enid said, stepping forward and holding out a hand to shake Sean's. "Sean, I'm pleased to meet you. There are high expectations in the executive wing for your project. From what I've seen, it is the only thing in the pipeline which would justify anywhere near the price paid in the acquisition of this company."

Her hand felt as soft and smooth as butter and he again had to drag his mind away from thoughts of how gorgeous she was. The fact that she was actively engaging him in conversation made things even worse.

"Nice to meet you," he eked out, wondering whether or not his unkempt appearance was turning the stomach of someone so beyond beautiful. Yet, she seemed genuinely interested in talking to him. What were the chances of that?

"I'm the new principal financial analyst," she continued. "Project Roadrunner will be one of the projects I'm working on as you prepare to go to market. Maybe we could grab lunch sometime next week once I've got my bearings?"

Sean wasn't sure if his discomfort was primarily due to his own ragged appearance or the fact that an attractive woman wanted to go to lunch with him. He knew it was work and not a date but, if Julee could see this woman, surely it would be clear to her that Sean's thoughts would struggle to stay pure.

"Sure, I'd love to get to know you and fill you in on our status."

Had he really said that? He'd love to get to know her? Inside he kicked himself. Certainly that wasn't appropriate for a man with a girlfriend.

"I'll shoot you an invitation sometime next week," she commented as she and DuWayne made their way toward the door.

He stood there alone as the final copy completed its stapling.

"Control yourself, MacCallister," he thought. "Don't screw up the good thing you've got."

He hurried back to his desk to lock everything up. He couldn't afford to miss the 7:00 train.

Chapter 7

Nick stole into the library, needing a good thirty minutes to finish his accounting homework. He knew the principles and had read the problems, he just needed half an hour to focus and get it all down on paper.

Making his way past the bookshelves, he found the library unusually busy with every seat taken but headed to the back corner, hoping to find solitude. He was disheartened as he saw in the distance someone who appeared to be sleeping at Nick's favorite table.

"No worries," Nick thought. "He's sleeping and there is plenty of room for me to do my work."

Then, taking two more steps, the smell got to Nick ten feet before he reached the table. It was the smell of cigarette smoke and stale body odor which emanated from the clothes and bushy black hair of the boy at the table. Nick nearly gagged as he stopped in his tracks.

Surveying the room a bit more, there was a small desk in the corner, just beyond his usual table. It was the kind with a small retractable arm which was designed for taking notes, not for laying out books, study guides and papers. Yet, it would have to suffice if he was going to get his homework done on time.

He held his breath as he walked past the sleeping boy, careful not to wake him. Then, arriving at the desk, he made his first attempt to get situated. Putting his workbook in his lap, he laid his paper out on the note-taking arm of the chair while balancing his textbook precariously at the edge of that same arm, cursing the stinky, sleeping boy in his mind for having chosen Nick's usual table.

Today's lesson was on the income statement. Nick started writing, looked up some reference material earlier in the chapter, and then continued writing. In a short time, he had filled half the page before realizing a mistake he had made in the Cost of Goods Sold section which would require him to go back and erase a significant amount of his work. As he bent to get an eraser from his backpack, his textbook took a nose dive off of the end of the note-taking arm, landing with a loud thud on the ground.

He swore under his breath as he bent down to pick up the book but, as he tried to get re-organized, he noticed the sleeping boy's head was still down on the table but his eyes were now staring intently at Nick beneath that mop of black hair.

Nick glared at the boy for a moment, suddenly wanting to get up and smack the kid for making the first half of his study hour miserable. But he returned his focus to regrouping and setting the textbook on his lap before beginning to erase.

Sensing the boy's continued gaze, Nick looked at him again. He had now begun to straighten up, not releasing Nick from his stare for a moment, causing the wrestler no small amount of agitation.

"Castle?"

Nick's name caught him by surprise. He recognized the voice before he recognized the face.

"Patron?" Nick asked back.

The dirty boy smiled.

Smell or no smell, Nick got up and walked over to shake his friend's hand.

"You're looking kinda skinny for a stud wrestler," Patron commented.

"Skinny or not," Nick shot back, "I can still run roughshod over your gimpy carcass."

The two boys stood and just stared at each other for a moment. Once close friends in junior high, life had taken the two in opposite directions over the past several years. While Nick's stable home environment had set a solid base for him to succeed, Patron had spent the majority of his high school years on the other side of the state, locked in juvenile detention – a "guest" of the state department of corrections and rehabilitation.

Despite Patron's comment, he himself didn't appear to be much bigger than Nick.

"Do you wanna use this table?" Patron asked. "That chair seems kind of small for your brainiac books."

Castle didn't feel like a brainiac, especially given that he was having trouble keeping up in several of his classes. Yet, he knew he would power through and pull good grades both to set himself up for college and to ensure that he remained academically eligible for wrestling.

"Yeah," he replied. "I don't suppose you're secretly an accounting wizard?"

"Never touch the stuff," Patron responded getting to his feet and pushing in his chair as Nick joined him at his table's opposite side.

"Are you going to stay?" Nick asked, a bit surprised by his friend's apparent quick departure.

Patron just shook his head.

"Gotta get to Job Corps," he commented as he walked away.

Nick wondered what the boy had been through. There had been dozens of stories and rumors but he hadn't talked to Patron since their freshman year and couldn't name one person who had. When the boy had gone to lock-up, he had essentially cut ties with everyone back home.

Suddenly, Nick remembered the sketchy details as if it were yesterday. Patron had failed to show up for the junior high conference tournament. Nick had been angry at first, assuming his friend was being a slacker again and had just chosen to skip the biggest tournament of the season but, when he didn't show up for school Monday, wild stories began surfacing that Patron had gotten involved with a gang, arrested for assault, caught selling drugs ... the list of offenses went on and on ... but none was confirmed until much later.

Staring until Patron finally disappeared out the library's door, Nick returned to his studies.

"Learn this stuff and get it right," he thought. "There won't be time these next four months to seek extra help."

First practice was only a few hours away.

Chapter 8

Nick looked around the practice room with a minor feeling of regret. The season officially started today, warmups were over and he suddenly kicked himself for not seriously considering Principal Skinner's offer.

The South team would be able to compete with Riverside overall with Nick at its core. Where things would be a bit lopsided was at the upper weights. Nick would shine bright at 152 or whichever of the surrounding weight classes Coach Nestor deemed fit for him to compete at. However, that was essentially the end of the line. 160 was currently slated as a forfeit weight as would 171 unless one of the Gull twins could find a way to cut. Above that were a handful of underclassmen and football players who had been recruited within the past few weeks.

Given Nick's prowess on the mat, this didn't leave him many options for practice partners. Clearly he would work with Coach Nestor and Tanner but Nick really needed others to mix things up.

He thought briefly about Bert and Chad, the Gull twins. They were both relatively strong but neither was especially agile or adept technically. Although, if he could work with them on technique, it may serve his own interest in building practice partners while serving the team ... if the two would be interested in learning. He really didn't know much about them beyond their names. The B. Gull and C. Gull on the backs of their respective warm-up shirts had inspired the Riverside team to nickname them Beagle and Seagull.

Tanner entered the wrestling room, saw Nick, and immediately went to the far side of the mats to warm up with some of the lighter wrestlers on the team. Nick had never really had a conversation with the boy and it looked like today would not be a day to change that. Yet, he would need Tanner and others to work with him day in and day out if he were to stay on track to compete for the title.

"Bring it in," Coach Nestor called.

Castle was the first to the center of the mat with the rest of the team in tow. He was eager to make a strong first impression on the team and his new coach. He knew that the man had won more state titles than any other wrestler in the city's history. He also knew that, from there, he had gone on to an injury-plagued college career and ended up right back at South.

"Our numbers are a bit light," the coach started. "If you have friends who have wrestled or may be interested, please feel free to bring them aboard. It will work well for all of us if we can increase our numbers."

The man looked around at the faces in the room.

"Unfortunately, we also had a setback on the coaching staff," he continued. "We had an assistant coach lined up who has apparently run into academic challenges at the university. Also, unfortunately, Coach Winger notified me this morning that he will only be with us through December."

The assistant coach in the corner didn't seem particularly remorseful about his choice to leave the team which immediately caused Nick to write him off as a potential ally. The boy mulled the overall coaching situation in town, and how Nestor was the only constant. He had coached for decades and, despite looking disheveled and unorganized, his tactical abilities put him eons ahead of Coach Kreitzer at Riverside and whatever minions the man would dredge up locally.

"We'll start with live wrestling. Pair up."

Looking around for a partner, Nick was immediately pleased by the coach's follow-up sentence, "Castle, you've got me."

The session would prove to be exhausting and exhilarating for the senior. Facing an aging state legend was a rush, especially when Nick found ways to get past the man's iron grip and defend himself against his coach's repeated takedown attempts. Yet, at the same time, Nick found no opportunity for offense against a tactician of his coach's experience. Clearly the man's interest in continuing to refine his skills had not ended after college. He had spent nearly twenty years teaching others while keeping his mind in the game.

Chapter 9

I love you, too. Drive safely," Sean commented before sadly hanging up.

It was the night before Thanksgiving and Julee had called from the road. She was plodding along on the eight-hour drive back to her parents' house while he was getting ready to spend most of the evening in his shabby little garage that came with his apartment.

He always felt great while talking to her and lousy when they hung up. The fun conversation lasted over an hour and he had plans for taking his mind off of the traumatic hang-up aftermath. Long-distance relationships are difficult and this one's issues were accentuated by his lack of reliable transportation and crazy work schedule. Julee had invited Sean to come home with her, but his project was nearing a major deadline and the giant corporation which had agreed to pilot the product had suddenly called a meeting for Thanksgiving Friday. They would be flying in half a dozen company representatives to discuss product features and expectations with a dozen leaders traveling in from the parent corporation of Sean's company. Thus, Sean would be spending Thanksgiving alone – probably in the office preparing a status update.

That was tomorrow. Tonight was his own.

He headed down to the garage. A thought of Enid crossed his mind but he quickly shook it out. After meeting her, it had taken the better part of a week to get the beautiful woman's image out of his head but she had eventually faded until earlier today when she e-mailed him about meeting for lunch. His 23-year old body chemistry kicked his thoughts into gear as soon as her e-mail appeared.

"No," he told himself with a furrowed brow. She was an amazing physical specimen, but Julee was the one who knew him inside and out and he was sure was his true soul mate. "Keep your mind on your girlfriend, or on your work, or ..."

He opened the garage door and his grin reappeared. There she was, his other love. He thought back to the first time he saw the machine, only five months earlier.

Sean had received a very vague voice message from his dad's former boss, Mr. Schwartz, while Sean and his sister Amy were home finalizing their dad's estate. Sean had gone to meet the old man at a storage facility he ran on the outskirts of town and had been guided to a beat-up storage locker which contained a large object covered with a tarp.

Grouchy Old Man Schwartz was giddy as he pulled Sean inside to reveal the treasure. Although he removed the tarp slowly, Sean recognized the make and model as soon as he saw the tail lights and gas cap. He watched in awe as Schwartz slowly revealed a rusted-out rear quarter panel, dented door, and primer-covered front quarter panel of a 1966 Mustang. Closer inspection revealed that the vehicle's insides were mostly gutted, no door panels, seats leaking stuffing, and an engine compartment which made the rest of the car look not quite so bad. The monster looked like Sean had felt a few months earlier and he could only sum up his feelings in two words, "She's beautiful."

Schwartz had explained it all, how the older MacCallister had purchased the wreck shortly after Sean had moved away, hoping some day that it would be a father-son project, rebuilding a car and a relationship at the same time. Sean was glad that the two had succeeded in the second half, the more important half, of his father's dream before the man had passed away.

After borrowing a truck and trailer to cart the thing home, getting the vehicle to a state of almost-roadworthiness had been a significant task that Sean had embarked on late at night and after work on weekends ever since. Occasionally, his former roommate Kelly would come up for a weekend and once brought their friend Dudley who worked at a service station and helped the two young men get the mechanical innards into shape – the car would at least start and move without assistance. He had even thrown in a pair of not-quite-as-bald tires as a "get well" present after Sean's surgery.

Sean would need to remove those tires to get on with this weekend's project – brakes. Like all other parts he used in the re-building process, the brake components were primarily assembled from pieces he had purchased through salvage yards and other second-hand sources.

He closed the garage door, flipped on the light and space heater, and was soon lost in his project, forgetting about women near and far and the work that seemed to consume his life.

Chapter 10

"What kind of a sadistic cretin schedules a tournament for the weekend after Thanksgiving?"

The thought angered Tanner for a few moments before he decided to re-direct his rage. "What kind of a heartless tyrant schedules his team to wrestle in a tournament the weekend after Thanksgiving?"

He shot his dad an irritated glance and continued jumping rope.

Of course, the man was wrestling with Castle, his new favorite, which annoyed Tanner to no end. Castle would have no problem making weight at 152 while Tanner had to skimp on the best meal of the year and was still five pounds over when practice started on Thanksgiving Friday.

"Just give me a week," the boy thought. "I'm going to challenge him to a wrestle-off and get my rightful spot back. No Riverside reject is going to take my spot in the line-up."

It was a day when nothing seemed to be going right. The first state rankings of the season had appeared in *The Herald* that morning and had listed him as fifth at 145.

"Fifth? Really?" He had thought. There was nobody at 145 who was especially intimidating. He looked at the other ranked wrestlers and pondered that they were all beatable. "Heck, somehow Oscar Black from Riverside had made it into the top eight and he was certainly no prize."

The lackluster nature of the 145 competition had lifted his spirits momentarily until he had looked at 152 where Castle's name topped the list.

"He won't win a state championship. Somebody will beat him," Tanner thought, "starting with me. I'm going to beat him in a wrestle-off next week. Then I WILL be the top-ranked 152-pounder in the state."

Nobody at 152 concerned Tanner any more than anyone among the 145-pounders. He would be a strong contender at either weight class.

"But what if someone cuts?" He had wondered. At 160, Chester Troftgruben held the top spot but rumor was that he was well over 170 when the season started. Another western-conference wrestler, Damien Trottier was ranked second. Trottier's reputation as a brawler off the mat overshadowed his prowess in the circle but, either way, Tanner didn't want anything to do with him. Hopefully Trottier wouldn't let Chester intimidate him and he would stay put at 160.

"I must have lost at least four pounds by now," Tanner thought as sweat continued to pour from his body.

"You go ahead and continue wrestling my dad, Castle," Tanner fumed. "I'll be saving a few surprise moves for you for next week."

Chapter 11

The discouraging look on his boss's face told Sean everything he needed to know as Sean described the situation.

"There are hardware and software changes that would be necessary to get to the new design. Between development, testing, potential rework ..."

"Rework?" the vice president got angry. "Why don't your people just do things right and there won't be a need for rework."

"Bryce, this is something that's never been done before, that's why we've started the patent process. There are going to be issues, that's why we have testers and a process for fixing issues."

"We don't have time for issues. We're behind schedule already. We've got a December 31 deadline to get this product into pilot and you need to deliver it, WITH these new features, do you understand?"

The only reason they were "behind" schedule was that the new management had suddenly forced an unrealistic timeline down their throats. Of course, Sean didn't expect any empathy from corporate management or Bryce at this point. Three days earlier, when the pilot customer had flown in for a meeting and demanded additional features, the engineering manager had made it clear that his team couldn't turn the additional requests around in less than three months. But the executives over-rode him and agreed to the customer's demands.

"We've already built prototypes. Adding features means that we would need to rebuild those with the new features and do so in the same timeline we had already committed to. There is a trade-off between features, quality, time and money. If they want more features at this point, it is going to either take more time or we'll have to sacrifice quality. I won't even ask about adding more resources and spending more money ..."

"Don't talk to me about money," Bryce growled. "If you don't deliver this on time, you're going to cost me and everyone else in this section of the office our annual bonuses. That's going to make you and your nerd team popular in a hurry."

"We can't wave magic wands and suddenly have a new product. This takes time ..."

"Well, spend that time on nights and weekends," Bryce snapped back.

"We already work every weekend and ..."

"Well, work more. The company floated you an awfully nice loan when you had your medical leave last summer. If you lose your job, you have to pay that back right away. I suggest that you don't give me any reason to fire you."

Sean bristled. The company had been very gracious in forwarding him over a year's worth of pre-tax salary to cover his medical bills from his surgery the previous summer and continue paying him during his absence. With all of his debt from his college years and medical treatment from two years earlier, the thought of losing his job and having that additional loan to repay immediately terrified him.

"Make it happen," Bryce said. "No excuses."

Sean could only nod and wonder how miserable the next month would be.

Chapter 12

Hey Crabtree, can you stay off of your back on Thursday?"

Tanner's comment irritated Nick. Alex Crabtree was a second-year wrestler at 119 and had made his first appearance in South's varsity line-up the past weekend. His giving up six points in each dual certainly hadn't helped the team. However, Tanner's salty appraisal of the smaller boy's performance wasn't what the kid needed to help turn his performance around. Especially since the first conference dual was on Thursday, just two days away.

"Nick, Tanner, are you ready?" Coach Nestor asked.

"Definitely," Nick thought, immediately sprinting to center mat. He waited patiently as Tanner took his sweet time walking over to meet him.

The two shook hands and the wrestle-off between South's only two undefeated wrestlers started.

The prior season, Nick had gotten caught off-guard in the first period when the two had wrestled in the Riverside-South dual and had quickly accumulated a five-point deficit before turning the tables and dominating the remainder of the match. He wouldn't let someone with such a significant chip on his shoulder do that to him a second time.

Today, Tanner surprised Nick by going upper-body. The counter-moves Nick had practiced for weeks on end at the past summer's camps immediately returned to him allowing him to block Tanner's attack, adjust his hip position, and throw the boy to the mat, quickly gaining the take-down and the lead.

"Two points."

"Time to learn some humility," Nick thought as he hooked a leg, wrapped up the boy's arms and, within seconds, had his opponent in a guillotine. He wasn't sure how to read the look in Coach Nestor's eyes as the man counted back points, but the look of pain on Tanner's face was unmistakable.

As he heard the coach's hand slap the mat, Nick immediately let his frustration with Tanner dissipate. If he was going to build camaraderie on this team, a good place to start would be to show this wrestler due respect despite the boy's attitude and the clear-cut nature of the wrestle-off victory.

"Starting with upper body was smart, I didn't expect that," Nick mentioned, looking Tanner in the eye and shaking his hand before his own hand was raised in victory by Coach Nestor.

A "yeah" and a shrug were all Tanner could muster as he glanced at his dad before walking away.

"This one might take a bit more work," Nick considered as he returned to continue practice.

Chapter 13

Sandi seemed nervous on the phone and Nick did his best to bolster her confidence.

"I'm sure you did great," he reassured.

"I can't say I was convincing. My character has to walk with a limp and I just don't know whether or not I pulled it off ... maybe I did too much ... I don't know. The time after tryouts drives me crazy. There is nothing I can do but wait until tomorrow when they announce the cast."

From what Sandi had told him about *The Glass Menagerie*, it was a small cast, certainly leaving reason for concern. He did his best to turn the tide.

"It's the other girls who should worry. You're the best actress Riverside has ever seen. Why would they put anyone else in that role?" It probably sounded like a boyfriend trying to elevate his girlfriend but Nick honestly believed every word of it.

"You must have some kind of tryouts in wrestling, right? Don't you get nervous?"

Nick thought about his wrestle-off from the day before. He had been slightly tense going into it but, unlike Sandi's situation, he took care of business and knew the result as soon as he heard the slap on the mat.

"I do," he admitted, "but I usually use that tension to help me prepare."

"Well, if I get in, it will be posted at the theater office after school tomorrow. Will you be around to console me if they reject me?"

"I'll always be there for you," he assured her. "We've got weigh-ins at 5:30 and the dual is at 7:00 but I'll drive to Riverside or to your house or wherever you need me to be. Just let me know."

"The cast list will be posted at 3:30 and then there is a mandatory meeting afterward for those who get in. If not, you'll probably find me in Smoker's Alley hanging out with a whole new crowd of folks."

Nick chuckled at the comment. Smoker's Alley was appropriately named as it was a few blocks away from school and a haven for smokers to light up during breaks. It was also the location for most after-school fights and rumored to be where a person would go who was interested in drugs and other illegal activities. It suddenly reminded him of Patron.

"You'll meet some characters there for sure," he responded. "Did I tell you about my friend, Patron? He's a smoker now ... he may be able to introduce you to the right people."

To call Patron his friend would still be largely accurate. The two never spent time together outside of school but Nick was making a habit of seeing the boy at the library every day during lunch. He had recently moved in with new foster parents but that was about all he had volunteered about his home life.

"Is he the boy that was in juvenile detention?"

Nick thought back to ninth grade when Patron had been taken away. It had been several days before any indication was given about his whereabouts or the reason for his disappearance. First came the news that he had been sent to the state's juvenile corrections facility and several days later, bits and pieces came out that he had been charged with assault. Still later, a friend of Patron's sister had confirmed that Patron had beaten someone with a baseball bat.

To Nick, who, at the time was about as naive as a freshman can be, it didn't make any sense. Patron certainly wasn't a saint; but, beyond the wrestling mat, Nick had never seen him have altercations with anyone aside from occasional verbal combat with those who ribbed him for being unkempt and having greasy hair. He had always held his own and Nick had never seen a need to get involved.

"Yeah, he spent some time there," Nick replied, "but he's actually a really good guy. I'm not sure exactly what led to them taking him away."

Nick thought some more about Patron, their earlier friendship, and the boy's current situation. Patron mentioned that he didn't like being with his foster parents but was having trouble getting a job due to his checkered past. Beagle had commented one day that every time he went to the mall, he saw Patron either wandering the halls aimlessly or standing outside smoking. He had been much more social in junior high and Nick was worried that Patron was quickly becoming a lost soul.

"Nick, you're so positive about people. That's one thing I love about you. Just don't let it get you into trouble."

The compliment had the strange impact of making Castle sad.

"If I'm so positive that Patron is a good guy," he thought, "why am I not doing anything as he spends all of his afternoons and evenings in solitude, making himself an easy target for trouble?"

"Thanks, Sandi. I don't have time to get into trouble right now but if I do, I'll want you to be involved."

The sweet girl laughed.

"I'll see you tomorrow one way or the other," she promised, "and if I don't make it into the show, you're committed to at least an hour for me to cry on your shoulder."

"I'll be there, despite the fact that there will be no need for you to cry. It will be time to celebrate."

The conversation continued for another twenty minutes before both said "goodnight" and turned their attention to homework.

Chapter 14

Sean sat across the table from Enid, completely mesmerized. He wasn't trying to be rude but could not take his eyes off the woman's face.

"The board meeting is in two weeks," she said. "We'll be going through the annual plan for next year. The performance of this business unit is really going to hinge on Roadrunner. I've been looking at the numbers and you're really showing some nice growth. I just don't want to put any figure in front of the board that is overly optimistic."

"Why did she have to use the word, 'figure'?" Sean thought. The only thing that was as distracting as this woman's face was her figure.

"There is a good chance that the guys won't be able to make their deadline," Sean started. "The customer was in over Thanksgiving weekend and requested extra features. I'm being told that we still need to deliver by the same deadline; but, as I've met with my team about this, there is serious concern."

"But is the 35 still doable?" she asked.

"35?"

"Your revenue projection," she clarified, giving him a document outlining the Roadrunner revenue forecast by month.

Sean hadn't been in the loop on any discussions regarding product revenue. As a Finance person, Enid's main focus was on the numbers and Sean's eyes bulged as he saw them.

"Roadrunner is expected to deliver 35 million dollars in sales next year?"

She only nodded, eyeing his suspiciously.

"35 million dollars?" he repeated. "I could see it ramping up to that over time but in year one with the timeline crisis we're currently in? Larry had told me last spring that we were looking to do five million or so in the initial year but nobody has ever mentioned these kinds of numbers. Where did you get those?"

"When your company was acquired last year, that was the figure that your management showed us in the strategic plan for the product. That's why the acquisition price was so steep."

Sean shook his head.

"How do we get to that?" he asked, diving into the numbers on the page as she spoke.

"US business-to-business sales is the biggest chunk," she clarified, her perfectly-formed hand with manicured nails pointing to the numbers. "But the smaller segments make up nearly 45% – US consumer sales are the bulk of that at around 25%, with European and Japanese sales accounting for the remaining 20%."

"Consumer sales?" Sean thought but stopped short of vocalizing. "This is a product designed for use within businesses. Who on earth is going to buy this for using at home?"

Yet, consumers were expected to make-up between eight and nine million dollars of the projected first-year revenue.

"We are SO DEAD," he thought.

Maybe he was wrong but he needed to check with Sales and Marketing to get their take on it. Seeing that they were the same people who had just agreed to everything the pilot customer had demanded that his team deliver without increasing his timeline, he wasn't optimistic that this was going to turn out well.

Chapter 15

Nick paced tensely, walking back and forth behind the row of chairs that held the South team. He tried not to look nervous during this dual ... but he was. He was very distracted and nervous.

The feelings had nothing to do with his match. That was already in the books, another Castle domination, pin 1:46.

No, tonight's distraction was in the bleachers.

As always, Nick had been overjoyed to see Sandi walk in. She didn't get to see nearly as many of his matches as he would like, so this rare appearance was welcome. What was unexpected was her companions. Sandi's friend Kendra was almost always with her, but tonight the two were followed in by two boys. One, a pretty-boy wearing fashionable clothing sat next to Sandi. The two had been talking through much of the dual ... and Nick didn't like it.

Nick trusted his girlfriend. He did NOT trust other men, especially ones who dressed like this kid.

Nick reached the end of the row of chairs and turned around to continue the circuit. One more match. One final meaningless match. South was down 15 – 32 so whether they won or not at 119 was irrelevant. He watched his teammate Alex Crabtree walk onto the mat, hoping for a quick South pin.

* * *

Nick made his way quickly through the line, shaking hands with the opposing team after the 15 – 38 loss. He listened to Nestor's pep-talk and was happy to not have mat-rolling duty this night. He needed to get to his girlfriend.

As Nick approached, Sandi was grinning from ear to ear at him. Kendra stayed with Sandi as the boys made their way toward the door under Nick's watchful eye.

Sandi ran up and gave Nick a hug. The two rarely kissed in public – and never at school. It was warm and reassuring to have her arms draped around him.

"You did GREAT!" she commented.

Looking at her radiant face, he found it difficult not to return her smile.

"I did alright," he replied sheepishly. Then, looking to the boys who were now leaning against the wall, near the exit, he followed with, "Who are your friends?" nodding in their direction.

He had tried his best to avoid any awkwardness in the question but was concerned that it radiated through his voice.

"That's Aiden and Martin," Sandi replied. "They're in the show with us and had never seen a wrestling match before. They asked if they could join us tonight."

Nick watched the two. When they saw him looking in their direction, they suddenly decided that it would be best to move toward the door.

"So you made the show," Nick commented. "I'm not surprised at all."

Sandi glowed.

"Yes," she replied, smiling from ear to ear. "I'm Laura Wingfield, Kendra plays my mom, Martin plays my brother Tom Wingfield, and Aiden is Jim O'Connor."

"Oh," was all Nick could manage to respond. The names meant nothing to him, having never seen *The Glass Menagerie*.

"Castle!"

Coach Nestor's shout was ill-timed.

"Coming, Coach!" Nick shouted back.

Nick gave Sandi one last big hug.

"Can you stick around a while?" he asked her quickly.

"I've got to get home. Aiden is giving us a ride."

Nick couldn't make his coach wait but suddenly had a very bad feeling.

"I'll see you on Sunday, right?" he asked.

"Of course," she replied.

As he watched her dazzling smile and the inner glow dancing in those blue eyes, he was concerned that she looked just as beautiful to others as she did to him.

Chapter 16

Sorry I'm such a downer," Sean said.

It was late Friday night and he had already fallen asleep twice while snuggling and watching a movie with Julee on his couch.

"It's ok," she replied, yawning. "After my Thanksgiving travel and the students acting out the last couple of weeks at school, catching up on sleep is a priority this weekend."

The two only got to spend one weekend per month together and were finding, sadly, that much of that time ended up being spent working. Sean tried to stay optimistic that, after Roadrunner was released, he would have more bandwidth for spending true quality time with her. Then again, her chaos wasn't likely to subside until summer.

"Students driving you nuts?" he asked.

Julee taught middle school English and was constantly amazed that she was able to keep her sanity. The kids were good kids but their bodies were going through changes, and they were on the fast track to adulthood. It was a time of confusion, acting out and high emotion, which she remembered well from ten years earlier and was dedicated to helping her students navigate through.

"It's not as much the students right now as the parents. I've got to find books that are more interesting for the boys. The athletes in particular just aren't connecting with a lot of the books our school has been using. Several of them handed in book reports in which it was very clear they hadn't read the books. When their grades reflected that, I got a visit from my principal because he had received so many 'hate' calls about me from parents. I have to grade fairly. I can't give free rides."

Sean thought back to his own adolescent years. He had often read as an escape, and books such as *The Outsiders* and anything else by S.E. Hinton resonated well with him. Of course, he did remember many of his wrestling teammates being less interested in reading than in more physical activities. He had no idea what young people would be interested in reading these days but was pretty sure that Hinton's books would stand the test of time. At the same time, he remembered how tough his junior high English teachers had been on him and his classmates. They were strict, but the students learned to write well in their classes.

"You're doing the right thing," he mentioned, eyes drooping as he kissed her on the cheek. "Helping them get into good habits now will make them better students in the long run."

"Well, then they're going to get a good start next week. I'm grading their tests this weekend. I hope you won't mind that it will take a few hours away from our time together."

"It looks like I'm going to have to get some work done as well," he admitted. The Sales and Marketing meeting had not gone as he had planned. The Sales VP had told him that, if Sean delivered the product as defined, her team would have no problem selling it. Then again, that was the same thing she had said two months earlier prior to the pilot customer calling for changes. Now, it was all up to Sean's team to move mountains and deliver the product by year-end.

He was beginning to explain some of these details softly when he noticed that Julee had dozed off.

"Sleep tight," he whispered as he pulled a blanket up over her. Within moments, he had said his prayers and drifted off as well.

Chapter 17

The South wrestling team's second conference dual wasn't pretty but, compared to the results of the first and the Thanksgiving weekend's triple-elimination dual tournament, it was gorgeous.

Nick was the only member of the team sporting a perfect five and zero record while Tanner was a strong four and one after being edged out in the closing seconds of his second conference dual match. Beagle had eked out two wins while Seagull and three other wrestlers were able to each win one of their first five matches. The three wrestlers to go winless dug a tough hole but it was the three built-in forfeits which hurt the most.

Missing wrestlers at 160 and 171 made life difficult for Nick. Tanner continued to avoid him both at practice and beyond, which usually resulted in Nick wrestling with Coach Nestor or Beagle. While the coach was more than a match for the talented 152-pounder, even though the smaller Gull brother weighed close to 190, Nick usually won convincingly.

In addition to lacking teammates as solid practice partners, Nick also noted minimal team chemistry and camaraderie. Most of the underclassmen looked to him more as a role model than a friend. Castle had begun building some relationships by getting a number of guys to go out for pizza after the dual tournament. It hadn't been easy to pull some of the guys out of their shells, yet he did feel that it at least provided an initial foundation.

If he could get the guys to feel like they were contributing to the greater good, maybe, just maybe, there was a path to improving as a team.

With gaps still needing to be filled and Nick's introvert personality not being especially conducive to recruiting others, the senior had pushed himself beyond his comfort zone and invited the one person he knew who had some, albeit a small amount of wrestling background — Patron.

The two connected regularly in the library at lunch. Patron's propensity to nap didn't do much for their conversations, but it did give Nick a good foothold on getting his homework done.

While the shaggy boy had initially come up with excuses why wrestling wasn't an option for him and then skipped going to the library the subsequent day, to Nick's surprise, Patron had shown up at practice two days later. Nick lent him a pair of wrestling shoes and the deal was sealed ... an under-sized 160-pounder had been added to the roster a week and a half before the big pre-Christmas tournament.

What Patron lacked in wind due to his smoking habit, he made up for in strength and grit. He wasn't muscular or defined by any means but had an iron grip and natural balance. Paired with his basic wrestling skills learned in junior high and some questionable tactics he may have learned in juvenile detention, his power and tenacity enabled him to go toe-to-toe with Tanner for a period before succumbing to exhaustion.

Nick didn't believe it was his place to get Patron to kick his smoking habit but, over the next week as the boy settled into a wrestling routine, he slowly decreased his tobacco use on his own.

"You know you'll need to get your hair cut," Nick teased him at practice one day, looking at the boy's unruly mop.

"Not going to happen," Patron assured him, "ever."

While Nick knew better than to insist, he also knew that eventually, a referee would have something to say on this matter.

Chapter 18

I saw your coach today."

Nick smiled in confusion about where Sandi would have seen the man as he shuffled the phone from his right ear to his left.

"Where did you see him?" Nick responded with the obvious question. He still wasn't great at conversation, but it did cross his mind how much better he had gotten at dialogue since he started dating Sandi ... she just made him feel comfortable and he found this comfort bleeding over when he talked to many other people now.

"He and your principal were coming out of Principal Skinner's office."

"They were at Riverside? Meeting with Skinner?" Nick asked, a bit confused.

"... and Mr. Kreitzer," Sandi concluded.

Nick froze. Why on earth would his coach and principal be on the other side of town for some kind of meeting? Wasn't that like fraternizing with the enemy? That may be a bit dramatic as Skinner had largely been good to Nick in the past, but Kreitzer was the enemy for sure. He stabbed Coach MacCallister in the back a year earlier and was angry with Nick for sticking up for his coach.

"Why?" Nick's question was more for himself but he heard the word as it inadvertently left his mouth.

"I'm not sure," Sandi answered. "They didn't really notice me. The principals both seemed to be in reasonably good spirits but your coach and Mr. Kreitzer both seemed a bit edgy."

"It has to be about me," Nick thought, feeling a bit tense. "But what? Is Kreitzer trying to get me in trouble?"

"I was just in the main office to pick up the reference letter the Superintendent of Schools had left for me for the Sorbonne," Sandi continued. "The four of them were wrapping up some kind of meeting just as I was about to leave."

Nick's stomach tightened again. He knew of Sandi's hopes of studying in France after graduation but now it looked more and more like things were getting serious. She had been wait-listed at the Sorbonne and they had asked for some more essays and references which she gladly provided.

It made Nick anxious that her aspirations were so contrary to his own plan to stay near home. If he could get a wrestling scholarship, certainly it would help pay the bills ... but that wouldn't make it any easier to be thousands of miles from her. He secretly wished she would stay home and just go to the University. They had programs that would let her study in France for a semester or a summer. Maybe, just maybe, that would be enough to satisfy her hunger for travel.

"Any word on when you'll hear back from the Sorbonne?"

"For international freshmen like me, they make their choices in late January."

"Well, they would be crazy to not let you in," he stated, trying to sound supportive.

Chapter 19

Tanner was literally running scared. He sprinted down the hallway of the domed stadium, terrified that his father would find out what he had done the previous night ... and its implications on his weight this morning.

The team had worked out briefly the prior day and Tanner had gotten a sweat going before getting on the mini-bus. His dad knew that he had been six pounds over when they started the practice. What he didn't know was that Tanner had skipped lunch to help keep his weight low. Having only had an apple and peanut butter for breakfast, he was famished by the time the bus arrived at its destination after its four-hour journey.

After quickly weighing in and finding himself still more than four pounds over, Tanner had resolved to get some sleep and get an early start in the morning but it wasn't meant to be. He was ravenous and his stomach was growling. He convinced himself that he would need energy for the following morning's workout, and thus embarked on a solo journey to the convenience store a block away from the hotel. Then, it happened ...

Tanner scoured the junk food aisles and ended up buying the bulk container of gummy orange slices, a one-pound bag of red liquorice, chips, soda and a bunch of other carb-loaded garbage your average goat would avoid. Feeling jittery on the way out of the store, the boy cracked, taking his purchases to the darkened area behind the store and gorging himself, telling himself that he would stop after the cravings were satiated but devouring well over half of his purchases right there in the back lot.

Now, twelve hours later and tipping the scales at nearly 150 pounds, the boy ran for his life. The thought of facing his father's wrath was even more daunting given the sugar hangover he suffered from. His whole body convulsed from the after-effects of the binge as he continued to dash down the halls, not having any faith that he would be able to sweat out the excess pounds in time.

Chapter 20

Y ou on weight?" Patron asked.

"Of course," Nick replied, putting on his sweatshirt.

Could there be any question? Nick had weighed just over 151 and would easily certify.

"How about you?"

"159 and change," Patron replied.

Glad that Patron's weight wouldn't be an issue, Nick momentarily pondered how Patron might perform at 160. Clearly, if the boy ran into Troftgruben or one of the state's other studs, it would lead to a very short match. Still, there may be other wrestlers with less experience who Nick's buddy could stand toe-to-toe with.

Even though he was far from being in wrestling shape, Patron had made the most of his week and a half of practices and was starting to purge some of the toxins and crud from his system.

The two boys dressed quickly and left the locker room, waiting for their teammates in the hall. They watched wrestlers of every size and shape, decked out in stocking caps, sweatshirts, jackets and multiple other layers, trying to shed those last few ounces.

A kid in a ski mask who was either exceptionally burly, wearing more layers than most, or both ran up to Nick and pushed him into the wall. Patron immediately stepped to his friend's defense before the perpetrator broke into a wry grin, pulling up his ski mask to reveal the face of Chester Troftgruben.

"How you doin', Bud?" Chester asked Nick.

Nick could only smile back at the sight of his friend.

"Much better than you apparently," was his initial reply. "I can't believe you have to run to make 160."

"Not today. I'm going 152."

Nick froze. He was sure that a look of shock and dread covered his face.

Chester didn't seem to notice. The golden boy pulled his ski mask back down and took off down the hall at a sluggish pace, calling back as he went.

"Gotta go," he yelled, "only ten minutes until weigh-in."

Nick didn't know what to do. If Chester was truly going to make 152, surely it would be the end of Nick's winning streak and possibly the end of his dream of becoming a state champion. He paced uneasily, ignoring Patron's jabbering to ponder solutions. Clearly he was too heavy to make it down to 145, he momentarily considered praying that Chester not make weight but it seemed wrong to call on God to the detriment of his friend.

As the minutes ticked away, Nick headed back to the weigh-in room, sick to his stomach.

"Get a hold of yourself," he thought, trying to restore his own confidence. "How could you have been so confident that you could beat Spegidos last year and now you're scared to death of Chester?"

The words were still going through his head when, in the background, he heard Coach Nestor's voice yelling.

"A pound and a half?! Are you kidding me?!!!"

"I ..." Tanner tried to defend himself before being cut off.

"I don't want to hear your excuses! We're already forfeiting two weight classes and now we have to give up a third because you don't make weight?!"

For someone who didn't consider himself to be intellectually quick on his feet, Nick surprised himself by immediately cutting into the conversation in a seemingly selfless way.

"Coach?" He asked, drawing the man's attention. "I'm fine wrestling up a weight at 160. It would give me some stronger opponents and push me a bit harder."

The man looked suspicious but didn't have reason to know why Nick might be fleeing 152.

"What about you, Patron?"

Nick stopped. He hadn't thought about what kind of a bind this might put his friend in.

Patron had an uneasy look on his face but, true to his form, he bucked it up.

"I can go 171," he responded tentatively, giving Nick a distrustful look out of the corner of his eye.

Nick was sure he would have to come clean on this at some point – to save his conscience if nothing else – but, for now, he would hide wherever he could to avoid having to face Chester.

Chapter 21

Nick sauntered out to the center-mat looking completely relaxed. His eyelids hung low as if he were half-asleep or in a trance. He entered the middle circle, stepped on his line, and stopped.

It was on this very mat and in this same semi-final round that a year earlier, having been forced up to 152 pounds, Nick had suffered his worst loss of his junior season, an absolute shellacking at the hands of Chester Troftgruben. As Castle looked to his new opponent, something echoed in the back of his mind. The boy was ten pounds heavier than Nick, his chiseled physique showed him to be significantly stronger than Nick, but in the end, it was what the boy "wasn't" that really mattered. The boy wasn't Nick.

A handshake and the word, "wrestle." He switched from relaxed to aggressive. Immediately, Nick was after his man, shooting, attacking, driving his opponent back, the larger wrestler soon realized that he was the prey. He was ranked third in the state at 160 and was not used to losing. As Nick took him down, it was clear that losing was to be his opponent's outcome that night.

It was a relentless, yet measured attack. Nick took the boy down, turned him to his back and held him past the five-count. When it was clear that a pin was not inevitable, he let the boy turn to his belly, let him go and started again.

The second chance from neutral position was even more Castle-centric than the first. Memories flooded into the boy from the past summer's wrestling camps at Iowa, the J Robinson camp, and several others. Nick had gone toe-to-toe with the top wrestlers from across the country ... and excelled.

"Forward," echoed in his mind. "No retreat! Let him dance. He can't escape."

Within seconds, Nick's opponent was once again on his belly, struggling to avoid being turned ... to no avail.

There would be no comeback. There would be no third period. Nick left an impression on everyone in the arena.

Ghosts of junior year disappeared as Nick shook his opponent's hand, had his arm raised in the air, and retired to mat-side to retrieve his warm-ups.

Chapter 22

Nick sat in an isolated area in the stands, taking a breather. With his headphones on, the boy was able to block out everything else from the world ... temporarily.

Having secured his spot in the tournament finals the previous night, Nick could have laid low, spending the day at the hotel or just watching wrestling from the bleachers. Yet, genetically, he couldn't. Nick had gotten antsy thinking about his title match. With the South team down to one assistant coach, he found himself seated in the corner of some of his teammates who had made their way to the tournament's second day, getting to see a number of wins and losses from the coach's chair.

The first loss of the day had been the most difficult. Patron had eked his way into day two due to an opponent having to default. Being a light 160-pounder, nobody expected the boy to do well at 171 but Nick was at mat-side for Patron's first match Saturday morning. It had actually turned out as nobody expected, being a close contest with the score tied with less than a dozen ticks remaining. Unfortunately, Patron had been on top and, in desperation to prevent an escape, he had clasped.

Clasping is one of those things that happens in the heat of the moment and only needs to take place for that long ... a moment. As the boy's sweaty opponent was trying to get to his feet, Patron had lost his grip and instinctively locked his own hands together to try to maintain control.

"Clasping, one point green," the referee had called and signed, locking his own hands to show the scorer's table.

Without enough time to score any points of his own, the dejected South wrestler pushed his opponent away, giving up another escape point as time expired.

It was a match that stung Nick. The boy felt responsible for having pushed his friend up a weight class. Ideally, Patron would be cutting to 152 instead of being a novice facing giants. Nick knew that "close" would not be cause for celebration but hoped that it would be sufficient to keep Patron engaged and on the team.

He walked with his buddy back toward the locker room, reinforcing what the bigger boy had done well.

"I lost," Patron said. "I clasped and it cost me the match."

"It happens to everyone," Nick had tried to console.

"When was the last time it happened to you?" was the frustrated reply as Patron looked Nick in the eye.

Nick really couldn't remember the last time he had been called for clasping and it was clear he wasn't doing a very good job of helping keep his friend's spirits up. After a moment of meeting his friend's gaze outside the locker room door, the two boys turned to head opposite directions ... Patron to the showers and Nick back to the gym.

This match and its aftermath was re-playing in Nick's mind as he noticed the wrestler in Riverside colors walking up the bleachers toward him. It was less the uniform than the way the boy moved that made Nick immediately recognize his former friend and teammate, Oscar Black.

Nick promised himself he would be civil. Although the two had bonded sophomore year as the team's outcasts, too many complications had been thrown in their paths since then. It started with Nick's general dislike for Oscar's attitude and work ethic but expanded to girl problems and eventually exploded when Oscar had refused to do anything to protect Coach MacCallister when the man had been wrongfully accused of purchasing alcohol for Oscar and subsequently fired. In Nick's view, Oscar had no honor.

"Hey traitor," the boy greeted Nick brusquely, immediately raising Castle's ire.

Nick stared at him for a moment, not really knowing how to respond beyond, "Hey."

"Sitting here with all of your friends?"

Physically, Oscar had changed significantly over the past two years, going from being a light 112 to 130 a year later and was now bulky enough to wrestle 145. The South wrestlers whispered that he was using steroids but it wasn't something Nick felt was worth bringing up.

"It had looked like a good place to avoid undesirables but apparently that was deceiving."

"Your girlfriend thinks I'm desirable, but then again, she gets around."

"Don't let him get to you," Nick thought.

"If you mean she gets around the state to see me win championships, you're right," Nick replied. "She'll be here tonight. Her whole family is driving in to see me and then take me skiing."

"She's been seeing some junior theater geek for a month now. They're inseparable. I've seen his car parked in front of her house twice this past week when her parents were away. She's probably slumming with you to get an extra Christmas present."

Nick's mind drifted back to the recent dual where the theater boys joined Sandi but didn't let any concern cross his face.

"Unlike you, Sandi's got lots of friends," Nick countered. "I'm sure all of them are interested in her, but she and I have already talked about this," Nick lied. "She isn't interested in anyone, and I'm not worried about any of them."

"You know how you can tell she's lying?" Oscar asked.

Nick only glared in response.

"Her lips are moving," Oscar finished, turning to walk away.

Nick continued to glare at the boy, showing no hint of being rattled at all.

"You're lucky you can hide at 145," Nick stated as Oscar plodded off.

Chapter 23

We lost another one."

Sean winced as Adam, his engineering manager filled him in on their staffing.

"The economy isn't great, but good people can always find jobs," Adam continued. "We can't work these guys every weekend and expect to not lose them."

"Who was it?"

"Danny."

Sean shook his head. He had gotten to know Danny pretty well. They had dug into testing and remedied a few bugs together.

"Any chance we can get him to stay?"

"He seemed pretty resolute, so I doubt it."

Sean would try his hand at getting the man to stay but wasn't optimistic. The thought of offering up some of his own paycheck to keep Danny on board crossed his mind but he was barely getting by as it was. Some companies would offer more money but in this big corporation, focused on short-term earnings, there were no additional funds available. Even if it had been an option, nobody was complaining about their pay. The hours were the issue. When people burned out, leaving became the default option.

This month, after expenses and debt payments, Sean had found a way to pay down an extra $150 of his debt and still tucked away $200 for buying Julee a Christmas present. Of course, that meant foregoing buying any additional parts for the Mustang.

"Is $200 enough?" he wondered. He had never been in this serious of a relationship before and he wanted to make sure that he didn't mess things up by being too conservative on gifts.

"He'll still be here until after Christmas," Adam added, bringing Sean out of his financial thoughts.

"That's good. We're going to need him," Sean replied. "Dare I even ask where we're at against the timeline?"

"It all depends on the current build. If the customer will approve it, this may be the last one."

Sean knew of some minor issues still lingering in the product but hoped that none were significant enough to cause concern.

Chapter 24

Sean enjoyed one final breath before the feeling of guilt set in. Enid's perfume still hung in the air of his office for a few moments after her departure.

"How could someone smell so nice all of the time?" the young man wondered.

As usual, he had been mesmerized by the flawless woman, even though the topic was an unfortunate one of project finances. She had such a friendly way about her and was so jovial. He was finding it hard to identify things to dislike about her. Yet, he was really trying hard as he couldn't bear considering that anyone else could be as wonderful as his Julee.

Initially, he believed that he could write Enid off as being conceited, but it certainly didn't appear to be the case. She never seemed to look down on or speak poorly of anyone and didn't even seem to quite realize how gorgeous she was.

If only the news she had come over to deliver could have been as delightful as the messenger, Sean would have gone into the weekend on a very high note.

Unfortunately, someone in purchasing had ordered some of the key structural components for the Roadrunner product based on the preliminary design before the customer had requested additional features. The costs of the components ran well into six figures. Sean suggested sending them back to have them retrofitted for the new design and, although Enid thanked him for thinking of options for reducing the financial hit, she doubted that the savings would be considerable.

In short, the product's sales plan was not achievable, development delays were likely to hold-up sales even further, and now expenses were running higher than planned. He wondered if he looked as exhausted and defeated as he suddenly felt.

Yet, the woman knew exactly what to say before she left and it even sounded sincere.

"You've really been given some nasty luck," she noted. "Why do I feel you'll find a way to turn this around and make it golden?"

After all of the beatings he had taken from management recently, it was reassuring to know that someone seemed to feel that things could work out. If only momentarily, his optimistic side returned.

"That's why they hired me instead of some inferior MIT or Stanford project manager," he joked.

Her brilliant smile in return was all he needed to see before she left him to ponder another weekend behind his desk.

Chapter 25

Nick was elated when Sandi and her family walked in the door. She ran to him and he caught her and gave her a big hug. He would have kissed her if not for the watchful eyes of her parents who followed closely.

"We're not late, are we?" the girl asked.

"No, the championship round starts in fifteen minutes, but I've got to get down there to stretch and warm up right away. My parents have saved seats for you in the middle section," Nick responded as he pointed to his parents' prime location in the stands.

He was a bit nervous for her to come just for this match. Damien Trottier was the de facto top-ranked wrestler at 160 now that Chester had moved to 152. Although Nick had edged the boy at one of the previous summer's wrestling camps, he knew that he needed to get his head into the game if he was to prevail today.

"Aiden came over to practice for the show and mom and dad were a bit delayed running some errands, so we were worried that we wouldn't get to see you before the big match."

Nick hoped it wasn't obvious when he cringed. After Oscar's comments that morning, he wasn't comfortable hearing about Aiden, especially when Sandi's parents were out of the house. Yet, the fact that Sandi would even mention the situation made him feel more confident that she wasn't trying to hide anything from him.

"We'll be ready to leave as soon as you're done," Mr. Davis commented. "The chalet owner knows that we could be late but I told him we'd make every effort to be there by 8:00."

Castle had never skied before but figured the brief outing would be a welcome break as he would get to spend time with Sandi and her family while at the same time getting extra physical activity on the slopes to keep him toned.

"I'm looking forward to having some downtime with you," Sandi commented.

Positioned behind her, her parents couldn't see how she raised her eyebrows at the end of the statement, getting Nick a bit more excited. He grabbed her and kissed her on the forehead before turning back to his preparation.

"I've got to get ready," he said, hoping that he could turn off the Sandi-related thoughts which were now percolating in his mind.

"Get focused and win this match," he thought. "If that doesn't happen, it could be a miserable way to start a weekend getaway.

Chapter 26

Nick's arms were so heavy and sore that he could barely hold them up as his opponent, Damien Trottier continued to attack. For the first time in months, a shot of pure fear penetrated Nick's spine.

Castle had raced out to a 4 – 1 lead in the first period, taking the state's top-ranked 160-pounder down twice but having difficulty holding the stronger boy down.

In the second period, Trottier had chosen "down" and Nick had immediately begun putting in the legs and working half-nelsons but found that his lanky arms were not working as well against an opponent of this size and strength. It was like trying to use a crow bar to move a steel pylon – the object just didn't want to move. As Nick wore down, his opponent earned a late-period escape to cut Nick's lead to two points.

Choosing down to begin the third period, Castle crawled, sat-out, scooted, and rolled, in attempts to get his larger opponent off of Nick's back. Yet with each passing second, the wrestler felt his energy disappearing. He felt Trottier's arm smack him in the right cheek and eye in a vicious cross-face. As he felt his own left arm being grabbed by his opponent's right hand, he instantly realized his options had become, "escape now, or end up on your back."

Trottier shifted to the right, setting up for a cradle but leaving Nick a split second opening to move to his left ... and move Nick did, shuffling and shimmying, left, left, left – getting his legs free and eventually turning to face his attacker and rise to his feet.

"One point green," the referee bellowed as the score changed to 5 – 2.

Nick valiantly tried to hold on to his three-point lead entering the final minute of the championship match but found his opponent's additional ten pounds and massive arms wore him down quickly. He pondered the look that must be on Sandi's face at this point. He had glanced up at the end of the second period and seen a grimace of pure horror. At that point, he promised himself he would not look up again.

Trottier pushed Nick out of bounds with 53 seconds remaining.

"Warning, stalling green," the ref cautioned him.

All the wrestler could do was look back in exasperation.

"What else can I possibly be doing?" the boy thought as he returned to center mat. Seeing the renewed confidence on his opponent's face as the two boys re-engaged, he realized there was only one option – be aggressive. He couldn't afford to give up a point for stalling and doubted that he could fend off a takedown for nearly a minute. He had to muster whatever power he had left and turn it into an attack.

The whistle blew and Nick shot immediately. It wasn't a good shot but had enough penetration that his opponent's sprawl and defense burned off another twelve seconds before the referee called a stalemate and the two wrestlers again stood to face each other.

Nick's arms were rubber. His only sense of feeling in them was some involuntary shaking as the two appendages begged for some rest.

As if sensing Nick's body's weakness, Trottier took a shot. Nick sprawled, using his legs and hips to ward off this new attack but it was only to last fifteen seconds before his opponent took him down hard, landing especially heavily on the right side of Nick's rib cage.

"Two points red," the ref bellowed and immediately followed it with, "work up, green."

With twenty seconds remaining, Nick knew that a stalling call and the subsequent overtime would result in roughly the same consequence as if he were to be turned to his back quickly – losing the match. Again, he pushed himself forward, looking for "up and out" any way he could get it. Trottier pounded him in the right side, completely taking the air out of the boy and causing him to collapse back to the mat. He felt Trottier move into position on top and pull Nick's left arm into a chicken wing. The arm put up minimal resistance; it was nearly limp. The best Nick could do was move his body in the same direction Trottier was pushing him to scoot across the mat and avoid being turned.

Nick battled for what seemed like an eternity. He fought to pull air into his lungs, but every breath created a shock of pain where Trottier had hit him in the ribs ... something was definitely wrong there. Despite Nick's valiant effort, his opponent eventually got the correct angle and leverage to make Nick flip to his back. The fog horn sounded.

Time stood still as Nick and Trottier both looked at the ref and the crowd got silent.

"No points," the ref remarked at once creating a pained sigh of relief from Nick and a verbose rally of complaints from Trottier's coach.

Trottier pushed Nick away as the winner lay in a heap on the mat. He couldn't take a deep breath without sharp pain shooting through his ribs but somehow managed to crawl to the center, struggle to his feet, and have his limp right arm raised momentarily before he doubled-over in agony. Coach Nestor helped him to his corner.

"Those cheap shots were garbage," Nestor told his wrestler. "They're trying to make like him falling on you was unintentional but he knew exactly what he was doing."

Nick's mind was swimming. He had wrestled in a lot of heated matches over the years but certainly had never spitefully tried to injure an opponent. It would have made him livid if his mind wasn't drifting back and forth between anger over the poor sportsmanship, concern over his injury and a quandary over what to do next.

This match had just been too close. For one more night, Nick was undefeated but how much longer could that streak possibly last against such heavy and powerful opponents? He was able to wrestle-up and win the third-most prestigious tournament in the state in front of the girl he loved, her parents and his parents. Yet, he had given his doubters from the western half of the state plenty of fodder. He would need to come up with a plan to stay on top.

The awards photo showed a broken-looking wrestler receiving the gold medal.

Chapter 27

Sean was dejected as he hung up the phone. It was a week before Christmas and suddenly, his Christmas plans had been thrown into disarray.

The original plan had been for him to take the train to Julee's where they would spend their first Christmas as a couple. He had no vacation days left and she had two weeks before school re-convened so she would leave for her parents' house on the twenty-sixth and he would return to long hours at work as he and his team raced to make their deadline.

Yet, in tonight's conversation, that had all fallen apart. Julee's brother and his girlfriend, who were also teachers, announced their engagement and were choosing to have a small wedding ceremony on the twenty-third in Julee's hometown. This enabled them to use their Christmas break for their honeymoon.

With Sean's sister Amy having moved to South Carolina, it now inevitably appeared that he would be spending Christmas alone. He suddenly longed for the previous year's tumultuous holiday spent with Amy in Wisconsin when he got to see his dad in the hospital. While Sean had left in an uproar after his dad suggested that Sean may be clinically depressed, he later came to see that the old man was right and that Sean displayed many of the symptoms of depression. A side benefit of his time in Alcoholics Anonymous and getting his life in order had been the relief of many of those symptoms.

For the first time, Sean momentarily questioned his relationship.

"Why do I have a girlfriend," he thought, "if we never get to see each other."

He tried to shake the thought from his head as he donned his coat and walked to his garage in a funk. Amy had sent him the letters F, O, R and D for his car's hood as a Christmas gift. They couldn't be affixed properly until he painted the car which would have to wait until the summer, so tonight he would work more on mechanicals.

Even if the car was an eyesore, his goal was to have its innards functioning so that he could drive it to see Nick wrestle in the state tournament. Six months earlier, he had sent the boy a postcard, promising to be there. While he had sent it anonymously to reduce the risk of being caught violating his restraining order which prohibited him from contacting Riverside wrestlers, he hoped that the message on it would make it clear that the card was from him.

His whole departure from Riverside and that point in his life seemed like years ago. How it could only be ten months seemed unreal. He just hoped that, once he got there, he could spend some amount of time talking to Nick without running into an unpleasant confrontation with Kreitzer. As enjoyable as it might be to face the man one-on-one and let loose on him, legal troubles and legal bills were the last things Sean needed right now.

He opened the garage door and turned on the light. He had a date with the car's radiator tonight and hoped beyond hope that it was in better shape than the alternator he had fixed a month earlier.

Chapter 28

The click of the key in the cabin door made Nick perk up and take notice. He craned his neck to see Sandi arrive, decked out in her cross-country ski attire. It was clear to Nick that it really didn't matter what the girl wore – shorts and a tee shirt, burlap bags or full winter survival gear, if he could see her face, he thought she was absolutely ravishing.

It certainly hadn't been the ski weekend the two had signed up for. Sandi and Nick's grand plan had involved lots of fun in the snow during the day and early evening hours and enjoying the hot tub at night. Nick's injuries allowed him to do none of the above. He just felt lethargic and sluggish as he loafed around in front of the TV.

"What's on?" Sandi asked, crossing to the room, stealing up behind him and kissing him on the head.

"You don't want to know," he replied.

In a cabin with few channels to choose from, Nick had struggled to find anything engaging and had finally settled on a show counting down the world's stinkiest animals. When skunks came in at number two, Nick checked his pits as a precaution. He was pretty sure that, after a typical wrestling practice, he could be stinkier than just about any other creature on earth.

Sandi plopped down on the couch to the right of him and he immediately winced and inhaled quickly. Terror crossed her face.

"Did I hurt you?" she asked.

"I'll be ok," he replied, continuing to grimace.

"Do you mind coming to this side?" he asked, patting the couch cushion to the left of him.

She complied ever so daintily and he put his arm around her, wincing again at the movement.

"Does this happen often?" she asked.

Not sure of the origin of the question, he could only respond with, "what?"

"Injuries; do you and your teammates get hurt often?"

"Oh, that ..." Nick replied. "No, not so much ... at least, not to this magnitude."

Nick realized that this was the first injury he had gotten since he and Sandi had started dating. Coach Nestor had diagnosed it as bruised ribs – painful but not season-ending like his broken ankle he suffered at the conference tournament his sophomore year.

He pulled her close and kissed her on the cheek.

"Are you sure you want to keep doing this?" she asked.

The boy was suddenly confused again.

"Snuggling with you on the couch?" he asked.

"No, wrestling," she replied. "I remember that you broke your nose last year and that you were on crutches when we were sophomores. It seems like all guts and no glory."

"All guts and no glory?"

"Yeah," she continued. "It almost seems like gladiators, going out there to injure each other but nobody in our part of the state seems to take any notice. Hockey games and basketball games are always packed, but I went to your match the night of my tryouts and there were a handful of parents and maybe ten other people there. Is it really worth all of the work and pain if nobody notices?"

Nick was taken aback. The question made his head spin a bit. What was he if he wasn't a wrestler? Who was he if he wasn't working toward his state championship? Who would he hang out with if he wasn't part of the wrestling team? He didn't even know what that world would look like. He couldn't give up his core identity. Yet, not wanting to cause a fuss, he moved to change the subject.

"The broken nose didn't happen during a match," he explained, feeling very uncomfortable. "The other ankle and rib injuries are just odd one-offs. I'll be good to go again in a couple of days."

It did occur to the boy that he had experienced more than his allotted share of bodily damage from his sport but he couldn't imagine any situation in which it would cause him to quit.

"This is about achieving my goals," he told himself, "not to become a celebrity."

The two spent most of the remainder of the afternoon in silence, watching TV. Their evening activities included board games with Sandi's parents. While it wasn't the active weekend he had planned, it did have the benefit of giving his ribs a rest. Yet, when the Davis family dropped him off at home the next day, he felt a bit hollow ... as if he had just squandered a major opportunity to expand his relationship with Sandi.

Chapter 29

Sean closed the overhead bin above his desk and packed some project papers into his bag. He figured he had just enough time to catch the final train home and had gotten enough work done that he promised himself he would not work on Christmas Eve or Christmas Day.

Having been in a bit of a funk for several days after learning that he and Julee wouldn't be able to spend the holiday together, the twenty-third had turned out better than he could have ever hoped for.

His college roommate and Beta Beta Beta brother, Kelly, had called him around noon. Sean ate lunch at his desk while catching up with his best friend for half an hour. Among the news that the man reported was that Nick had placed first at 160 pounds at the pre-Christmas tournament.

"160, wow," Sean thought. "How could he have bulked up that much over the past year? The kid must be huge."

The two promised to talk both of the next two days to keep each other's spirits high.

Then, toward the end of the day, Enid had stopped over, just to say, "Hi."

The two had met regarding Roadrunner the prior day and she had asked about his Christmas plans. When he told her that he would be alone, she had felt really bad. Sean was surprised at the amount of sincerity in the woman's eyes as she told him that, if she hadn't already committed to leaving town, she would have invited him over for Christmas dinner.

"If we're both orphans," she said, "we should stick together. Nobody should have to spend holidays alone, especially Christmas."

Today, Enid's follow-up had been to surprise Sean by showing up with a small wrapped present which, upon opening it, he found to be a key ring with the Mustang logo on it.

"Is that the kind of car you said you're working on?" she asked. "I don't know much about cars but I hope you like it."

"I love it," he said as his heart filled with gratitude. "Thank you so much."

Feeling suddenly awkward about getting a gift from this gorgeous woman, he continued, "... but, I didn't get anything for you. I'm sorry, I ..."

"Your Christmas present to me is that you didn't get me anything," she cut in. "I don't need anything."

Sean was amazed that the woman was suddenly appearing to be as beautiful on the inside as she was on the outside.

She had said an additional, "Merry Christmas" and had disappeared down the hall, leaving Sean with a warm heart as he navigated through a few more hours of work.

When he rushed out to catch his train that evening, he felt very fortunate to have friends and colleagues around who were looking out for him.

Chapter 30

*S*ean looked at his Mustang key ring sitting on the table in front of him at Whitey's. Nick had switched to water when the two had started talking but his drinks from the afternoon were still in his system, causing him to chatter away, very different from the quiet kid that Sean had remembered.

Based on the boy's story thus far, Sean was very pleased that the first third of Nick's senior wrestling season had gotten off to such a strong start. Noticing the key chain reminded him of happy times that winter in his own life while the boy was still pursuing wrestling glory.

"I feel like I've been doing all the talking," Nick said as it finally dawned on him how much he had been yammering. "Tell me about you these past years. What have you been up to? Why did you decide to shave your head in the winter? It's cold out there."

Sean shuddered a bit, not wanting to dampen the mood but it soon occurred to him that his initial reason for making this trip was to reconnect with Kelly. A big part of that was to give him a trusted ear to confide in about his messed-up life.

"Um, the hair," Sean started slowly. "Nine months ago, my wife got severe head trauma in a terrible car accident and ended up in a coma. They shaved off all of her hair so I started shaving my head too at that time."

"I'm sorry, Coach. Is she doing better now?"

Sean had to clear his throat a few times before continuing.

"Um, well, sadly, her condition hasn't really changed. We transferred her to a facility an hour south of here in late August as her parents wanted to have her closer to them."

"Coach, I'm sorry, I shouldn't have asked ..."

"Nick, you didn't know. You shouldn't feel bad about asking. It's probably good for me to talk about it. Living in an apartment in the big city now, I don't seem to strike up real friendships as easily as I once did."

Nick sat quietly as Sean continued.

"She was my glue. She was my angel and always found new ways to take care of me. She bought me a new suit for Christmas last year, just before the accident. She said that it is always important to have a good suit around. I've been fearing the worst lately that I may end up needing it for her funeral."

The two sat in silence for several seconds before Sean turned the conversation back to what would hopefully be a more uplifting topic.

"Anyway, I'm feeling old talking through those kinds of problems. Let's get back to your senior season. What happened in January?"

Nick still felt sheepish but was happy to change the subject.

Chapter 31

Two more reps, Castle," Patron coaxed.

From his place on the bench, Nick forced up 185 pounds for a fourth, then struggling, pushed out a fifth rep.

It felt good to get back in the weight room again. While there was never a good time for an injury, his timing was about as good as it gets. He was ginger with his ribs at practice the week leading up to Christmas but was largely recovered by Christmas Eve, a week after the injury occurred. Upon revelation of Nick feeling "healed," his dad had agreed to get up at 3:00 a.m. to drive Nick home from their Christmas gathering at his cousins' farm so that the boy could make it to the morning weight-lifting session. He knew that Nick's toughest matches of the season were still ahead of him and wanted to support his son in preparing for them.

As Patron took his turn on the bench and cut the weight down to 165, Nick pondered how much Chester might be able to bench press. The western conference wrestler had the chest of an NFL full-back. Surely he must be able to push out reps at 225 each.

"Nice set, Nick. Let's see what you can do Patron," commented Coach Nestor as the boy donned the bench. With a determined look in his eyes, Patron began his reps.

"All the way to your chest and then up slowly," Nestor advised before turning his attention to Nick as the spotter.

"Were you doing your final sets at 185 in the off season?"

"Yeah," Nick confirmed. "But it felt easier then."

"You're working your entire body harder day in and day out," the coach confirmed. "You probably have some overall fatigue, even if you're not cutting weight. The amount that you can lift may drop but that doesn't mean you'll be less prepared for what can happen on the mat."

"But his guns are there for intimidation," Patron joked as he strained under the weigh.

Nick jokingly flexed his biceps in response, making the coach smile.

"Those guys don't fear his strength. They fear his inner being. Anybody can put a piece of metal on a bar and, by lifting it enough times and eating right, become stronger. It's the mental strength and aura that make him come out on top."

Patron finished his final rep.

"Nice form, Patron," the coach commented.

Nick thought about the body types of many of the state's toughest competitors. Clearly, he had beaten some muscular opponents over the years. Just because they packed more physical power didn't mean much when they stepped out against someone with Nick's tenacity.

Chapter 32

Tanner felt humble.

Usually his dad's speeches just made him resentful but, for some reason, the one after pre-Christmas tournament weigh-ins actually resonated with him.

"Castle saved your butt," his dad had said as the tongue-lashing began. "He is the only reason you are wrestling in this tournament!"

This time, instead of being cross, Tanner acknowledged, albeit only to himself, that what his dad was saying was true. Tanner screwed up and Nick and Patron each took one for the team, moving up a weight class to ensure that South could have better representation. In doing so, Castle silently made it clear why the team was stronger with him than without. Surely only a true leader would volunteer to move to a heavier weight in a tournament like this with so much at stake.

The younger Nestor had competed relatively well at 152, placing sixth. It was eye-opening to him as he wrestled some of the state's best and took a significant thumping in the quarter-finals at the hands of the number three seed. He was amazed by how that same competitor got pounded a day later by Troftgruben in the finals.

"He must be super-human," Tanner had thought as he watched the golden boy win the championship match 13 – 4. He wondered if even Castle could stand a chance against that kind of power and immediately decided that perhaps 145 wasn't such a bad place to be. Making the weight wasn't easy but at least the lighter weight class didn't have the same kinds of goliaths.

Over the next week as Castle was on the mend, Tanner swallowed his ego and even made an effort to talk to both Nick and Patron. To his surprise, Nick seemed to welcome him without animosity. Patron was harder to get to know but, after practice one day, the sullen senior had opened up and was getting a little bit goofy with the guys.

Just after Christmas, most of the team seized the moment and, not having to weigh in for nearly a week, went out for pizza. A little pizza goes a long way in team-building efforts. Practices that week, twice per day during the break, suddenly seemed bearable.

"Maybe this team has a chance," he thought after their first dual win of the season in a New Year's Eve tournament thanks to impressive showings by himself, Castle and also Patron, the Gull brothers and a handful of others stepping up when it counted. "Maybe things could still come together."

Tanner entered the new year with an improved attitude and outlook.

Chapter 33

Thanks, Mrs. Davis, that would be great. Please have her call me when she gets home."

Nick hung up the phone, grabbed his books and went to his room. He had a lot of homework to do as mid-term finals approached. Early January was always tough like that but this year seemed especially daunting – so much on his mind.

While school was supposedly the most important thing he needed to focus on, it also seemed the easiest for his brain to avoid. Every time Nick began hitting the books, his mind wandered. Sandi filled his thoughts most often, but wrestling was a close second.

"Oh, Sandi ..." he muttered sadly under his breath. His occasions for seeing her were few and far between. Outside of school, if he wasn't at wrestling, she was at evening play rehearsal and vice versa. She had spent most of Christmas break out of town with her parents. This, of course, gave Nick plenty of downtime to let his ribs recover but did nothing for helping his disposition. Being away from her made him tense. To make things worse, half the time when she told him about rehearsal, Aiden's name would come up. Nick wasn't sure whether he should read that as something that should calm him – if Oscar's assertions were true, Nick assumed she avoid mentioning the kid – or concern him – if she indeed was interested in the boy, it was likely that he would be on her mind regularly as he seemed to be.

Wrestling was his main escape. When he was at practice or preparing for matches, he was largely able to focus and keep his mind off of his insecurities related to Sandi.

Tanner actually started to open up to Nick, and the two began pairing up at practice. The boy was wrestling smart and was a welcome addition as his technique was far better than that of Patron or the Gull brothers. He gave Nick a solid option for times when Coach Nestor was not available.

"Study!" the boy commanded himself as he opened his Pre-Calculus book. As of yet, only one small college had contacted him regarding a potential wrestling scholarship; but the school's college of business wasn't accredited, so he didn't see it as a likely option. He wanted to go to the university and stay close to home, but having not placed at state as a sophomore or a junior, the recruiters had not yet reached out to him. It would likely take winning a state championship to get their attention. Perhaps Kreitzer had been right at the end of his junior season. Maybe Nick had needed to wrestle, more than the team and coaching staff had needed him.

He wondered what the recruiters may be saying about him. Was he not naturally talented enough? Too skinny? Did his injuries spawn rumors of him being too fragile? Did not wrestling at state as a junior tag him as unreliable?

He knew for sure that Chester had already been contacted and was being pursued by several schools – even with lack-luster grades. Nick would have to keep both his GPA and his undefeated record up to ensure that there were no stumbling blocks when the recruiters eventually did call. Certainly, it would only be a matter of time.

His return to Riverside for the annual South-Riverside dual was only two days away. There was nobody his former school could put on the mat against him who would present any kind of challenge. Oscar had been a surprise, placing fourth at 145 at the pre-Christmas tournament. Nick found himself hoping that Riverside would move the kid up to 152 so that he could teach him a lesson about implying that Sandi was anything less than perfect.

The circle was now complete; he had found a way to return to thinking about Sandi again.

Eventually, he would get focused and resume his studies again ... but for the time being, he pulled out a picture of Sandi and himself at homecoming. Despite all that he had to be thankful for, there remained lots of work to be done in every area of his life.

Chapter 34

At work, Sean finished the old year and began the new year right. After a major push, his team delivered Roadrunner, tested and approved on New Year's Eve and the pilot customer took twenty beta units for its on-site testing that same day.

Enid stopped over and congratulated him when she returned to work the first week in January.

"I knew you could do it," she said and touched his hand.

A stream of exhilaration and guilt immediately swept through him. She had only touched his hand, but he had liked it – perhaps too much.

"Is she flirting with me?" he pondered. "It seems like she's interested, but I can't find out," he thought. "I've got a girlfriend."

Given his and Julee's lost time over Christmas, he was catching the Friday night train the first weekend in January to go visit her. They would exchange gifts and have some much-needed one-on-one time. Distance is tough on relationships, but Julee was worth the extra effort.

Yet, he looked at Enid and was still enamored.

"Beauty is only skin deep," he told himself. For some reason, his mind floated back to foster care in his youth. He swam with a boy whose mother had hit him with a hot frying pan, melting the skin on the boy's upper back. Some of the other kids had kept away from the boy, but he and Sean eventually became close friends while the "good looking" kids had treated both of them badly.

Then again, Enid was proving to be more than just a pretty face. She sincerely seemed like a good person and someone who would be a steady partner in a relationship.

"Thanks again for the keychain," he commented, showing her that he was now actively using it. "It really brightened my Christmas. You're wonderful."

He shocked himself with the last couple words. Had he really just told this woman that she was wonderful? How will she react to that?

"Flattery will get you everywhere," she commented and flashed him a big smile before turning to leave.

Her perfume stayed in the air for several minutes, and his mind remained on her even longer.

Chapter 35

Nick burst down the hall at a full sprint. Getting to the end, instead of slowing down, he leapt up the flight of stairs, clearing five steps in his first leap and subsequently bounding up the remainder of that flight and the adjacent flight three at a time.

His compatriots weren't even close. He was a good five seconds ahead of Tanner, and Patron was far enough behind that the competitive side of Castle was pondering trying to lap his friend.

"No."

He shook his head while sprinting down the second-level hallway. He couldn't do that to Patron. There had to be some other way for Nick to up his game without negatively impacting his friend's confidence.

The answer dawned on him as he approached the stairs. Slowing down to avoid descending the stairs too quickly and risk turning an ankle, Nick meandered to the bottom and waited with his back to the staircase, listening and waiting for his friends.

Tanner quickly descended to the landing behind him. As the younger Nestor approached the bottom of the case, Nick yelled, "Jump on."

Obediently, Tanner jumped on Nick's back and the boy took off down the hall again, carrying an extra 150 pounds and pushing his legs to their limits. Reaching the end of the hall, he again bolted up the stairs, this time, just two at a time and then one at a time, nearly cracking under the extra load. He could hear Patron on his heels as he trudged toward the apex. Three stairs from the top, Patron passed Nick who let out a smile.

Upon reaching the second floor, he dropped Tanner and fell to a heap on the floor, his legs wobbling and his chest heaving.

"Buddy carries, Castle? Seriously?" Tanner remarked.

"We ... did them at ... camp ... this summer," Nick forced out. He knew the extra effort would prove valuable in the long run, but now he was exhausted.

Typically packed with students between classes, the halls were extra-wide leaving plenty of room at 6:30 a.m. for the wrestlers to meander, hands behind their heads, elbows pushed outward to help open their chests and breathe deeply.

"What drives you, Castle?" Tanner asked, trying to gain some perspective.

"Inadequacy," Patron replied before Nick could get a word in.

Nick rewarded the boy by driving him into the lockers as Patron laughed. Yet, there was a grain of truth in Patron's comment.

"I'd phrase it as dedication," Nick said. "I'm dedicated to living up to my brother's reputation and the expectations that people are placing on me to bring home a state title."

Tanner was silent for a moment, as if the conversation was resonating with him personally. It suddenly occurred to Nick that the underclassman was in his same boat, living in a much bigger shadow.

"Do you get some of that pressure to follow in your dad's footsteps?"

Tanner only nodded.

The three milled around for only a second or two more before Nick continued.

"... then let's get going. They're not going to give us state titles for our looks."

He took off down the hall again and the other two, slowly at first, followed in tow. It would be the first of many such morning work-outs. Sometimes the cast of characters expanded, and other times it was just Nick and Tanner.

What was clear was that a bond was starting to form, and the boys were pursuing their individual quests together.

Chapter 36

Sean hugged Julee and held her close for another moment. Then, he boarded the train and headed home.

He was emotionally exhausted. He got to spend so little time with his girlfriend and the weekend had gone by far too fast. As the train began to roll, he looked out the window and saw her put her palm to her lips and blow him a kiss ... and then she disappeared from sight.

It was becoming abundantly clear to him that relationships were hard work. When she had picked him up from the train station Friday evening, it was nothing like the movies as lovers race through the crowd to meet each other. It was two young adults, worn-down by a week of work and travel, scrambling to find each other, get bags and figure out a plan for the weekend.

The biggest part of that plan was in getting Julee's classroom ready for her students' return.

"I don't really feel that I can count on anyone at school to help me with this," she had commented.

Sean silently empathized. Since moving, he had not developed the kinds of close friendships he had fostered throughout his high school and college years. At the end of the workday, his co-workers went home to their families, out with their friends, or out to happy hour in clusters. With the exception of an occasional appearance at after-work social outings, Sean spent most of his extra time either at the office or working on his car. Meaningful friendships just did not seem to be in the cards.

"You can always count on me," he had replied, and thus ended up spending his entire day Saturday at her classroom and a significant portion of Sunday helping with other projects at Julee's home.

They exchanged Christmas gifts on Saturday night and, while Julee seemed to like what Sean had gotten her, he LOVED his present from her. She had found an automotive technician and had purchased a bumper-to-bumper tune-up and diagnostic check for his Mustang. He only needed to get the vehicle into good enough shape to get it to the technician who would fine-tune everything from there. It would certainly give him some peace of mind on the twelve-hour drive to see Nick wrestle at state.

Having been apart for well over a month, Sean initially felt more like Julee's guest than her partner. It had taken the two until Sunday to start settling in to being together. The afternoon hours in particular were warm and fun. But before he knew it, he looked at his watch and had to hurry back to the train station.

"Can this really last?" he mulled as the train picked up speed.

He had two and a half hours on the train and plenty of downtime at his place to ponder that very question.

Chapter 37

Had Nick had more than an instant to react, he would have taken time to smile and relish the minor victory. As it stood, that victory was short-lived.

Wrestling Coach Nestor at practice, Nick had found a rare opening, taken a beautiful single-leg shot, and after two months of trying, had finally gotten a clean takedown on his coach. Then, less than ten seconds later, the self-proclaimed 'Old Man' had escaped, gone on the offensive and gotten a takedown of his own.

Nestor was relentless. Each time Nick changed his position or went for a new move, his coach was already there to not only block Nick's defense but further his own offense. Nick couldn't figure out how the man could be so phenomenally quick.

The end of the drill found Nick on the losing end again but prepared with questions.

"How do you think and react so quickly?" the boy asked.

"The thinking was done years ago," the man said with a smile. "That saves me time now when all I have to do is react."

Nick's confused look was all the coach needed to continue.

"You need to work on combinations and forming habits. You are technically sound, in great condition and counter well for someone your age, but you need to develop the ability to continually think three or four moves ahead. If I grab your wrist, what do you do? What three ways could I possibly respond to your countering my wrist-grab and what do you do to counter those?"

The fog started to lift and Nick nodded lightly.

"I used to keep a notebook with various combinations in it. I started it on Christmas break my junior year and completely filled it by the end of the season. I studied that thing and each day at practice would try new combinations and add to it. It got to be that everything in that notebook, and eventually the notebooks that followed, became second nature. Once something becomes a habit, it is harder to not do it than it is to do it. Your body just naturally reacts to a situation without your mind needing to take time to ponder it."

Nick nodded. On days that he missed Riverside's facilities and reputation, and his friends, it only took conversations like this with such a knowledgeable coach to help him see that he had made the right choice.

The boy created and filled in the first four pages of his combinations notebook that night.

Chapter 38

Nick walked in the main student entrance of Riverside high school flanked by the Gull brothers, Tanner and Patron. He had an odd feeling of sadness and resentment as he and his teammates got to the first hallway. Beagle continued straight into the commons area before Nick directed him to turn left into the hallway.

"Are you sure?" Beagle asked.

Nick just looked at his teammate with a stare that made the boy fall in line. Nick had trod this same hallway hundreds of times to wrestling practices and gym class. There was no arguing that he knew the shortest route to weigh-in.

Another batch of South wrestlers strode in behind them and followed in silence. Nick's unusual amount of stoic silence sent a message to everyone. This was not a friendly visit. This was business.

Nick didn't take the time to find his way to the theater to visit Sandi. For the next two to three hours until he wrestled his match, he would remain focused. If she chose to come watch the dual, he would be pleased but he couldn't let her draw his attention in any way. In a battle of two struggling teams, Nick needed to deliver six team points. Nothing would stand in his way of doing so.

Chapter 39

The Star Spangled Banner ended and Nick walked over to give Patron a word of encouragement. 152 was to be the first match of the evening and Patron would be filling that slot. The boy had shed several pounds and Coach Nestor knew, as did Nick, that he would match up well against Riverside's 152-pound grappler.

Nick patted his teammate on the back as the boy stepped onto the mat. Patron had a look of intensity in his eyes and appeared ready. Having won two of his four matches at 160 since the pre-Christmas tournament, he was improving quickly and was rightfully confident as he strode out to face a Riverside opponent with a losing record.

"Nick Castle!"

Nick turned to see a group of four elementary school boys he had coached the prior spring. They lived in the Riverside district but were still holding up signs in support of their former coach which read, "Go Castle Go!" and "Castle = Mr. Wrestling."

He smiled and gave them two thumbs-up before returning his attention to the 152-pound match.

"Maybe this isn't such a bad crowd," he thought as he pondered the boys. Principal Skinner had found him after weigh-in and had reminded Nick that he continued to be a role model for the younger students. Castle promised that he would continue to act as such regardless of the colors he wore and the school he attended.

With Patron winning handily, Nick's tension was beginning to abate. If Riverside didn't default at 160, Nick knew that his opponent would be Freddie Watrud. Nick had gotten to like Freddie the prior season and promised himself he would not take the boy lightly but would still efficiently and cleanly deliver South the six team points which could be the difference between the team winning and losing.

Patron's major decision started the team off strong with four team points and put an extra spring in Nick's step as he pulled off his warm-ups and walked onto the mat. He was on the verge of giddiness; clearly his anxiety earlier in the day about returning to Riverside had been for naught.

As Freddie emerged from the pack of Riverside wrestlers, Nick noticed Oscar at the front of the group, waving to Nick and then pointing to the stands.

"Wow, even Oscar's in a good mood tonight," Nick thought as he allowed himself to smile, assuming that Oscar was pointing to the elementary school boys from earlier.

Nick then noticed Kreitzer's attention turn in that same direction and the man gave a thumbs-up. Something suddenly seemed off to Nick as he glanced back at the stands to see what was drawing everyone's attention.

The highly touted wrestler's blood ran cold as he looked in the stands and, just four rows above his young followers, noted a very different banner. Tim Parks, who had bullied Nick his sophomore year, and a couple of other guys Nick didn't even know, were holding up a large sign that cut the wrestler to the core. The boy felt provoked and betrayed as he absorbed the bold letters and their unmistakable message.

CASTLE IS A TRAITOR!!!

A moment of shock and weakness left an empty spot in Nick's soul, which was quickly filled with bitterness and anger.

"Someone needs to pay for this atrocity," the boy thought.

As he shook Freddie's hand, it became very clear to Castle who that "somebody" would be.

* * *

The next ninety seconds of Nick's life were something that he did not remember. His upbringing forced him to completely black them out.

Freddie had been a teammate of Nick's a year earlier but, at this point, was the only outlet for Castle's rage.

Within three seconds of the opening whistle, Nick had shot a single-leg and finished aggressively, driving Freddie hard into the mat. For the following minute, he was lost in a frenzy, completely dismantling the younger wrestler, earning back points and giving up escapes only to drive his hapless victim into the mat once again.

On the verge of winning by technical fall, Nick fulfilled his promise to deliver six team points, stacking the unlucky Riverside wrestler and holding his shoulders to the mat.

After having his hand raised in victory, Nick did not acknowledge the combination of cheers and jeers which echoed throughout the Riverside gymnasium. His mind was a wreck. He needed an escape from the hundreds of onlookers who filled the stands.

The closest option he found was in pulling on his warm-up top and hiding his head and face in the hood. He was ashamed, not only of how he had been singled out, but by how he had reacted in response.

Chapter 40

Tanner fought valiantly from the bottom, milking an 8-5 lead over Oscar.

The South team had lived up to expectations, giving the historically stronger Riverside team a run for its money. The team score was tied going into the final match at 145 – the only match of the evening featuring two ranked wrestlers.

"We could actually come out of this with a win," Nestor thought. It wouldn't be a glorious win given that neither school was even able to field a full team this year but a win over your biggest rival at any time is a good win.

"Thank goodness Castle is on our side," his thoughts continued. "He could have dismantled anyone on the South team the way he beat that Riverside kid, which would have resulted in a clear Riverside victory had he remained at his former school.

Still early in the third period, Tanner suspected that the match was far from over. Oscar's strength had caught him off guard and made him imagine that the steroid rumors may be true. Yet what Black brought to the mat in power, Nestor countered with skill and balance. That left endurance as the final battleground as the match waned.

Tanner knew that if he wound up on his back for a five-count that Oscar would get three points and the match would be tied. He couldn't let that happen. If he could get to his base, he could position himself for an escape or possibly even a reversal. A win here would position him to move ahead of Oscar in the state rankings which would be incredibly valuable going into the upcoming Capital tournament.

Careful to not expose his back, the boy got his arms under him but immediately felt Oscar trying to insert a half-nelson. Tanner attempted to press his arms in tight to his body, but his opponent had already gotten penetration below Tanner's right armpit and began working to get a better angle.

"Not today," Nestor thought while trying to free his arm but soon realized that Oscar was straightening out the appendage.

"If he controls the arm, he'll put me on my back."

In desperation, he fought to get loose but found Oscar's grip ever-tightening on the right arm.

Intent on not being turned, he tried to pull his arm away but found it in an awkward position behind him with Black pulling it up and in the wrong direction.

A brief look of horror crossed Tanner's face along with a yell of agony as he felt and heard the shoulder pop.

The referee immediately stopped the match but it was too late. The shoulder was separated and all Tanner could do was lie face-down in pain.

* * *

Nick watched as his teammate lay helpless in the middle of the mat, surrounded by trainers and coaches. The referee had awarded the match to Oscar via injury default, but the smirk on the boy's face after his hand was raised told Castle all he needed to know. The Riverside wrestler showed no concern for his opponent and no remorse.

"That was flagrant brutality if I've ever seen it," Nick thought angrily.

The crowd clapped when Tanner was able to get to his feet, but the mood of everyone on the South team had soured.

As Coach Nestor directed his team to return to their locker room, the Riverside wrestlers began heading in the same direction to their own lockers.

"I guess they'll have one less loser at the Capital tournament," he heard Oscar tell a teammate, loud enough for the nearby South wrestlers to hear, as he disappeared through the locker room door.

"Talk smack all you want, Oscar," Nick thought. "There will be a surprise waiting for you in the capital city ... and it won't be a pleasant one."

Chapter 41

Sean looked at his watch and then at Jeremy.

"We've got to wrap this up," he mentioned. "My 11:00 will be here any minute."

"What is that one about?" Jeremy questioned.

"Enid from Finance is stopping by to go over the financials for the Roadrunner phase two plan."

"I think I'll stick around," Jeremy said. "She is SO HOT!"

"Settle down," Sean chided him, getting irritated. "Don't talk about other employees like that. You're going to get slapped with a sexual harassment suit."

"You don't think she's hot?"

"Drop it," was all Sean could say. Jeremy had just verbalized Sean's inner thoughts from the past several months but it all seemed so dirty and inappropriate coming from this wild colleague.

Jeremy got his things ready, stood up, and suddenly Enid was in the doorway to Sean's workspace.

"Ready?" she asked as she entered.

With her eyes on Sean, Sean noticed that Jeremy took the opportunity to check her out top to bottom.

"Of course, come on in," Sean replied.

Behind Enid, Jeremy mouthed something to Sean that Sean didn't catch but he was sure that it was inappropriate.

She sat down across from him and the two began to dig through the numbers. Despite a few hiccups, the pilot was generally going well and, while Sean still doubted that the revenue targets were anywhere near achievable, he had heard that the sales team was getting some good interest; so, at minimum, there should be some dollars coming in the door.

Yet, the main topic at hand was expenses for phase two. With the first phase being more than a $100,000 over budget, Sean knew that he and his team would need to find places to reduce spending over the next several months to offset the past issues. It wasn't the kind of exercise that most people enjoy, but they went through all areas with a fine toothed comb.

The half-hour meeting stretched to an hour and then an hour and a half before they were able to determine which costs could be eliminated. Some were straightforward as Sean knew that the members of the team who had left the company would still take time to replace; and thus, their salary dollars would go unspent. Beyond that, his bare-bones budget did not have much room. He found a few thousand dollars of savings by reducing the number of demo units they would build, but there weren't many other good options.

"I hope management doesn't start considering my position and salary as opportunities to reduce costs," he commented as they wrapped up, still a long way from balancing the numbers.

"If they want to get the product any time in the next few years," she commented back, "they should keep the people in place who are contributing to getting it done."

It was nice to know that he at least had one backer.

"Do you want to grab lunch?" Enid asked.

Sean was a bit shocked by the comment. He worked with a bunch of introverts which meant he typically ate lunch alone at his desk. Jeremy was the one exception but he could be more than a bit obnoxious, so it was becoming rare that Sean would eat lunch with him.

"Sure," Sean replied cautiously. It felt a bit awkward to be going to lunch alone with Enid, but the company cafeteria certainly wasn't a place where they could be looked upon as having a date.

* * *

People can learn a lot about each other over lunch, especially when that lunch stretches to over an hour.

Sean had always been intrigued by how a woman of the current generation could be named Enid and was floored when he found out that she had chosen the name herself. It was the name of her great grandmother who had taken care of her during much of her youth but had passed away while she was in high school. Her name had been Jennifer until that time, but she had changed it as soon as she turned 18.

It was another thing that the two had in common since much of Sean's youth was spent living with grandparents due to troubles in his home. He was starting to feel like he and Enid had a kindred bond. While they chatted, it felt like they were the only two people in the world and that she felt the unique bond as well.

He silently chided himself on the way back to his desk. He was becoming too close with this woman, and while it felt right, it didn't seem appropriate.

"What if I had met her before I met Julee?" he pondered briefly but quickly cut himself off.

He would not let his thoughts go in a direction that could hurt his girlfriend. It just wasn't right.

Chapter 42

Nick still felt a bit sweaty but, in general, he was feeling good.

In less than three hours, he would be leaving for the Capital tournament to defend his title. It was fifth period, Castle's free period, and he had used the time to go to the wrestling room, run and jump rope.

The boy had weighed 148 before the workout started and felt that the extra activity was exactly what he needed to ensure that he could still eat that evening and then lose whatever water weight was necessary in the morning before weigh-in. He would need to make scratch weight at 145 so, for the first day of the tournament, he would be giving up two additional pounds to his opponents.

"Why on earth would anyone cut weight if they didn't absolutely have to?" Nick pondered.

Chester had seemed absolutely miserable on the phone the previous night. Secretly, Nick had hoped that the boy would return to 160, but Troftgruben had resolved to cut to 152 and win the state title that had eluded him at that weight class the year before. Thus, he was pushing himself far below the weight that most would consider healthy for him.

Yet, running from Chester was only one of two reasons Nick was cutting. After Oscar's intentional injuring of Tanner at the dual a week earlier, Castle wanted to ensure that his former teammate didn't bring home gold at the Capital tournament. Likely being seeded fourth, it wasn't beyond reason that the mouthy kid could get lucky enough to slip into the championship and somehow pull an upset.

"Not while I'm alive," Nick declared, picking up his pace. Then, realizing that time was getting short, he pushed another twenty jumps at double-speed before hanging up the rope and starting toward the door which, to his surprise, opened from the outside when Nick was still ten paces out.

"... in serious need of some upgrades," Nick heard Coach Nestor state from the hallway. Yet, the first face that appeared was not that of his coach, nor was the second or third.

Nick froze as he suddenly stood face to face with Riverside's Principal Skinner, South's Principal Ohnstad, and another man whom Nick recognized from the Riverside corner earlier that week at the dual. The four men each had the "cat caught eating the canary" look on their faces as they suddenly stood staring at the sweaty boy.

"Nick," Coach Nestor began, "I didn't realize that anyone was in here."

"Cutting weight, I see," Principal Ohnstad seemed to be trying to turn the conversation from whatever the men had been discussing. "Gentlemen, I believe you know Nick Castle, one of our current stand-outs."

"It is good to see you again, Nick," Principal Skinner stated, reaching out to shake the boy's sweaty hand. "As I mentioned on the phone, I am very sorry for the poor taste of some of our students during your match. I assure you that we have reprimanded everyone involved and taken extra care to ensure that it doesn't happen again."

Nick just looked blankly at the man, being too intimidated to ask the obvious question of why people from Riverside were in South's little wrestling room.

"Nick, this is Coach Gasperini," Skinner continued. "He is taking over head coaching responsibilities from Coach Kreitzer whose sole focus will now be the administrative needs of the team."

It didn't solve the mystery of why the men were there but knowing that Kreitzer was no longer in charge lifted Castle's spirits a bit.

"You go and get showered," Nestor directed the boy. "Don't be late for class."

The men stood in silence until Nick complied. Something was going on and it made him nervous. He wasn't sure how long he could wait to find out what they were up to.

Chapter 43

On the brink of exhaustion, Nick stepped on the scale.

Cutting weight had been about as difficult as Nick remembered. He found himself following the advice he had given Tanner over the past couple of weeks. He continued to eat healthy foods which kept his digestion in good shape and had fit in some extra workouts over the past few days. Then, the morning of the tournament, he had broken a sweat and then piled on the clothes, run and jumped rope until he soaked two layers of sweatshirts.

Forty-five minutes before weigh-in ended, he felt he had given pretty much all he had left but when he checked weight, he was still over by more than a quarter-pound. It was then that he had run into Chester Troftgruben in the hall. The boy was still more than a pound over and looked worse than Nick felt.

"Do you want to run together?" Nick had asked, donning a dry shirt and pulling on his winter jacket and insulated leather mittens.

Chester was in a sour mood. Few things can taint a person's disposition more than dropping ten pounds over a handful of days and Troftgruben was currently the subject's poster child. Yet, sweating out the extra weight with someone else was better then doing so alone. Thus, he accepted Nick's proposal with only minor additional signs of irritation.

They ran in silence and Nick pondered their plight. Nick was predominantly cutting weight to stay away from Chester at 152 while either one of them could move up to 160 and immediately be ranked first in the state. It was insane that the two undefeated grapplers seemed to be torturing themselves for no reason.

The minutes ticked by and their pace ground slower. Neither would give up despite nearing delirium. With five minutes remaining, they checked weight. Nick made scratch weight at 145 and would benefit greatly from the extra two pounds the following day but Chester was still a few ounces over. His coach looked at him with aggravation and his eyes traveled upward to the boy's sweat-soaked hair.

"It's time to get rid of your mane," the man growled.

Finding a pair of bandage scissors and showing no mercy, he began chopping off blonde locks, one after another until all that was left of the boy's usual coifed mop was a mangled mess.

Barely able to stand upright, Troftgruben stepped on the scale. It registered 154 on the nose, causing Nick to ponder how Chester could have possibly made scratch weight a month earlier.

Both dehydrated, they left the weigh-in room to gorge themselves and leave concerns about the second-day weigh-in for 24 hours.

* * *

Nick stood at mat-side, waiting for the match to be over so that his quarter-final match with Oscar Black could begin.

The two boys had been in a stare-down just minutes earlier, which Oscar had ended by commenting, "With your gimp physique, I see your shoulder coming right out of that socket."

Castle wasn't intimidated by the remark. He had watched Black wrestle so many times that he knew exactly how to methodically approach beating the kid.

The match ended and Nick ditched his warm-ups and pulled up his singlet straps. While he tried to keep the perspective that this was "only a match," it certainly seemed bigger.

How many times had Oscar belittled Nick over the years? Nick was flooded with memories, first with the boy telling him he was too much of a coward to ask anyone to dance as a sophomore. This moved quickly to the time when Oscar had asked Sandi to dance during their junior year and dovetailed right into the boy implying that Sandi was cheating on Nick this year. Even without the boy's involvement in Coach MacCallister's firing and tearing on Tanner's shoulder, there was plenty to make Nick livid.

The wrestlers shook hands, the whistle blew and Nick was immediately in for a shot. To his surprise, Oscar also took an immediate shot and the boys smashed heads with Oscar's forehead catching Castle right in the nose and eye.

Nick saw stars as the pain surged briefly and shock took over. The impact was harsh enough and the head knocking loud enough that the ref stopped the match and sent the two dazed grapplers back to their corners to be checked for concussions.

Blood appeared from Nick's nose but his cognitive senses were fine. With some cotton to stop the bleeding, he returned to the center of the mat and was relieved that Oscar would do the same.

"Already made you bleed," Oscar commented as the two faced one another again.

This time, when the whistle blew, Nick did a much better job of setting up his attack. He led his opponent, locking up and letting him believe he may find an opening. Then, quickly, he set up his shot and this time achieved deep penetration and drove Oscar to the mat.

As the ref signaled for the takedown and two points, who his opponent was and their past differences suddenly disappeared. None of that mattered. What mattered was that Nick was on the mat to represent his school and win the match.

While Oscar was significantly stronger than Nick remembered from the prior season, that didn't matter either. The stronger boy spent much of the first period on his back as Castle found opportunities to turn him, earn points, re-position, and turn him again.

Leading 11 – 0 going into the second period, Nick chose the neutral position and, again, took the boy down within the first ten seconds. Then, exposing Oscar's back again, Nick gained a technical fall with a 16 – 0 win in under a period and a half.

Coming back out of his wrestling mindset, Nick looked into the eyes of his former friend as he shook his hand and then had his arm raised by the ref.

"I'm going to kill you, Castle," Black remarked before the boys returned to their coaches.

"After that match, you may want to save your threats for others," the ref interjected.

At the end of the day, the match didn't change anything. Nick was still undefeated but awkward, Oscar was still Oscar, and there was a place in the world for both of them.

Chapter 44

Nick was in absolute shock as he stood at mat-side, dripping with sweat from his match and watching the waning seconds of the 152-pound semi-final. His tattered mind returned to a conversation with Chester on the warm-up mat an hour earlier.

"They mentioned us on the 6:00 news tonight," Chester had said with a big grin.

"Really?" Nick questioned.

"Yeah, they ran some footage of the quarter-finals and mentioned that, since Condit and Lattegaard both lost, me and you are the only two undefeated wrestlers left in the state."

Nick was dumbfounded and briefly pondered what he might look like on TV. He could understand why they would clamor for footage of Chester. The boy looked like a young Robert Redford and, even without his blonde locks, his infectious smile and chiseled chest would make for good highlights. Nick, however, was certain to look gangly and awkward. He suddenly hoped that the saying about the camera adding ten pounds was accurate.

"Lots of out-of-state wrestlers will make the finals. I think they're looking for some in-state guys to come out on top."

Nick only nodded at his friend's words. The tournament's competition committee had done a great job of luring in top teams from five other states, creating a tournament with fierce competition. Wrestlers from afar made it to the semi-finals in every weight class. Nick's opponent was Steve Sandstead, a former teammate of Spegidos from West Clay, but Chester would be facing the Oklahoma wrestler Nick had beaten in the 140-pound title bout a year earlier. Surely the golden boy would pick up a win, but Nick was hesitant to guarantee his own victory.

Sandstead was certainly no slouch. At 18 and 1, his record would be strong enough to earn him the top seed in most tournaments. But this was the Capital tournament and he had Nick deciding to cut weight and two nationally-ranked wrestlers from out-of-state all still alive vying for a championship berth. No Doubt, he was hungry to topple Nick for his own gratification and glory in addition to wanting to see Nick fall due to his brother Ron's handling of Spegidos in the prior year's state title match.

"They're going to interview me after the championship match tomorrow night," Chester continued. "A reporter already stopped by and asked that I meet her by the awards stand. I got my hair fixed in case they film during the semi's tonight."

"Better you than me," Nick thought, feeling mixed emotions of jealousy and relief that he hadn't been asked to be on camera. He wasn't sure he could accept an interview at all before actually winning the championship. Then again, Chester was always brimming with confidence for a reason – the boy had already won a state title as a sophomore and had not lost a match this season.

"How great would it be if the camera crew would just film me getting a championship trophy for Sandi to see?" Nick thought. As long as he didn't have to speak, perhaps he would be just fine.

Chester's haircut comment made Nick pause and notice that his friend must have paid significantly to have someone re-shape his hair after the coach's butchering earlier that day. It was no longer long and wavy but it was certainly more stylish than the mop on Nick's head.

The boys' chatting didn't last long. Nick had wandered off for some alone-time to get into focused wrestling mode for his big match. If he and Chester were to remain undefeated and represent their state, they would need time to prepare mentally.

Yet, an hour later it appeared that the preparation was for naught. Nick was aghast as he watched the 152-pound semi-final. Having just eked out his own victory, 5 – 3, he had expected to watch Chester man-handle his southern opponent similar to the way Nick had dominated the same boy a year earlier. However, the scoreboard told a different story.

Time was waning and Chester was down 10 – 6. The muscle-bound boy simply looked like he had no energy or enthusiasm for finishing the match. A final tilt in the last 15 seconds looked promising, but his Oklahoma opponent rolled through after less than two seconds, avoiding nearfall points and securing the win.

Castle watched the time tick down and then walked away, not fully believing what he had just seen. He could hear Chester's coach as his friend walked off the mat.

"No more 152," the man ranted. "You looked weak and he gassed you. You're 160 from now on."

Nick didn't stay to talk with Chester, knowing his friend would be in a foul mood. Cutting weight and losing for the first time in a long time tended to have that effect on people.

Chapter 45

Nick felt giddy. He had repeated as Capital tournament champion with a 5 – 4 victory over a nationally-ranked, out-of-state wrestler. In doing so, he retained his status as the last remaining undefeated wrestler in the state.

Making weight had been much easier that morning with the extra pounds being allotted. The only disappointment was that he hadn't seen Chester. His friend hadn't been up running again in the early morning hours, and later Nick noticed that he defaulted his next match. He didn't know the boy's teammates well enough to ask them about his whereabouts and thoughts crept into Nick's mind that Troftgruben had been injured in the semi-final. It would certainly explain his lackluster performance.

Nick walked toward the awards stand thinking of this most recent victory as well as his victory a year earlier after which his mom had taken a picture of him with Coach MacCallister. He made a mental note to bring a copy of the picture to the state tournament this year in case his former coach showed up to watch him wrestle.

"Nick! Nick Castle!"

The unfamiliar woman's voice calling his name interrupted his thoughts and caused the wrestler to look around. He quickly filled with fear as he saw a very attractive 30-something walking toward him with a camera crew in tow.

"Nick Castle, I'm Vivian Hotchkiss from the 10:00 news. May I have a word?"

The senior wanted to run but feared that the cameras were already rolling and he would make headlines if he turned and sprinted away.

"Nick, you're the only undefeated wrestler left in the state. How does it feel to be so successful among such strong competition?"

His mind was blank. All Nick could do was stare at the camera and think about the thousands of people who were sure to see this broadcast.

"Good," he finally squeaked out.

"Just good?" Vivian continued, waiting for a better answer.

"Uh, really good," the frightened youth clarified.

Vivian clearly realized that she was going to have to do most of the talking.

"You've won the two biggest tournaments so far this year and done so at two different weight classes, fifteen pounds apart. Is that common?"

Nick's head was spinning. He hadn't really thought about things in that way and couldn't come up with the name of another wrestler who had done the same in recent years.

"No."

"Do you have any predictions for state?" the interview continued to his chagrin.

What on earth kind of prediction was she looking for? He wondered.

"I'm gonna work hard," he answered, not really considering whether or not the answer related at all to the question.

Looking at the woman's impeccable hair, the thought crossed his mind that he must look his worst. He had just wrestled a six-minute match and then thrown on his warm-ups. His hair was probably completely unkempt and he had gotten a bloody nose during the match. He wondered if there was still blood residue under his nostril. Instinctively, he began rubbing his upper lip and the bottom of his nose with the back of his hand.

"We're sure you will, Nick," Vivian continued. "Thank you for talking with us."

"Thank you," Nick replied.

"This is Vivian Hotchkiss reporting from the Capital City wrestling tournament. Now back to you, Lisa."

The light on the camera went off and the woman immediately walked away toward the camera man with a grimace on her face. She mumbled something to the man and walked away, not looking back at Nick again.

Chapter 46

I didn't feel like it."

Chester's response surprised Nick.

"I was eight pounds over and I didn't feel like cutting when the best I could do was plow through the wrestle-backs and place third, so I didn't."

"Didn't your coach flip out?"

"Yeah, he had already told me that I couldn't wrestle 152 anymore because I looked weak so, in a way, I was letting him be right for a change."

Nick thought back to the time as a sophomore when Granger cut him from varsity, saying it was too late for Nick to make weight. He still believed that he could have dropped those extra ounces before weigh-in had he been given a chance. In many ways, it brought to mind Coach MacCallister's comment on integrity from a year earlier, "Say what you're going to do and then do it." Nick had never missed making weight after agreeing to do so.

"So are you going to wrestle 160 the ...?"

"By the way, you looked like a gomer on TV," Troftgruben interrupted.

Nick cringed. He had been proud to wrestle so well but his confidence dropped when he saw himself on that night's news clip. He looked like a bumbling idiot.

"Yeah, it wasn't my best moment," Nick admitted.

"They should have been interviewing me," Chester continued.

Nick would bet big money that his cool friend would have performed well in the interview. It was just one more reason that Nick should avoid time in front of the camera. Others could just do it so much better.

Then again, back home, Nick had now been invited to appear on a local news broadcast featuring the top high school athletes in several sports. If he were to accept, he would need to find a way to look more self-assured.

The boys continued talking for a while and Nick felt more and more confident that, without Chester at 152, it would be the best weight class for him to finish his senior season. He was scheduled to have a large French dinner with Sandi's family the following Friday evening, so cutting to 145 probably wouldn't be the best option for him for next Saturday's tournament.

Chapter 47

I've never been much good at public speaking," Nick commented as Sean sat back and smiled.

He wondered if Nick was always this chatty now or if alcohol was playing a major role. The younger Castle brother had always had the reputation of being insecure around people, and thus keeping to himself. Yet, his story made it sound like he had blossomed his senior year – even having a girlfriend.

Insecurity and fear are odd things. Everyone has some amount and they can either be debilitating or forces which drive people to greatness. The way Nick's story seemed to be heading, he would fall into the latter category.

Then again, for all the progress that Nick had made, the young man still had some idiosyncrasies that were evident. For starters, he always kept his right hand under the table. It jogged something in Sean's memory that there had been something wrong with Nick's right hand the last time he had seen Nick, but their time together had been so brief and harried that details escaped him so many years later.

Quirks aside, Sean had been grateful that he had run into Nick this evening. His life had fallen into shambles in the past nine months and he suddenly had nowhere to turn. His wife's inability to recover and an ongoing fight among her family on whether or not she would want to live in a coma had made him desperate enough to leave the hospital and head blindly into a winter storm.

Castle kept talking and MacCallister was glad. He had a lot to get off his chest but certainly didn't want to burden Nick with it. He had spent far too much time soul-searching and realizing how nothing physical and tangible is permanent.

All people physically die. It is a sad fact that human bodies degenerate over time as do all other "living" things. All jobs change or disappear. He thought of how his HR department referred to those hired by his company as "permanent employees" but the average career-span at his company had been under five years. Even mountains crumble over time.

Yet, emotions and the spiritual side of life seemed to be ongoing. Love, fear, elation and remorse have always existed outside of the physical realm. While humans attempt to seek unending joy by doing things and having things, they rarely seem to realize that the happiness they seek has been with them all along. It is easy to forget that during times of great loss.

Losing a job and potentially a loved one in quick succession can impact a person's perception of who they are and the value they bring to the world. Sean liked to think that he was stronger than that ... but in recent days, he wasn't so sure.

He sat back and continued listening to Nick, needing to hear that things had turned out fine, but feeling that, as in all journeys, there must have been bumps along the road.

Chapter 48

Your boy may look scrawny and geeky but the kid can wrestle," Kelly commented. "I saw him on the news last week and he couldn't put a full sentence together, but they said he's the only undefeated wrestler left in the state."

Sean smiled as he listened.

"Good for Nick," he thought. "He'll be at state when I get there for sure."

Sean only had one match of Nick's in his current apartment. Somehow, the recording of Nick's junior year pre-Christmas semi-final had ended up in MacCallister's possession. It was the only match that season in which Nick had gotten absolutely throttled. It lifted the young man's spirits to know that his protégé had not been on the wrong end of a similar thumping this season.

"State is the last weekend in February?" Sean asked.

"No, they moved it up to the third weekend this year – some kind of scheduling issue," Kelly replied.

In some ways, the earlier weekend would be better. Sean had needed a weekend getaway for quite a while now. However, it reminded him that he needed to get his car in for that tune-up and that he had one less week to get that done. He hadn't seen Julee in nearly a month so any of the next three weekends would be an option and a good chance to see her.

"He's down at 145 now," Kelly continued.

"145? Really? How did he cut all the way from 160?"

"I don't know, Sean. He'd look better if he put on a few pounds. Of course, he might be better served to spend some time at Toastmasters to work on his public speaking."

"Watch it, big guy. That's my protégé you're talking about."

It dawned on Sean how much he enjoyed his occasional chats with Kelly. Other than his newfound friendship with Enid, he really didn't have anyone in the big city that he discussed anything other than work with at all.

"You should move down here," Sean offered. "A change of scenery would be good for you and it would be fun to see you more than a couple of days a year."

"I can't leave here," Kelly countered. "I just got my dream job tending bar at Whitey's and the Beta Beta Beta's still need a big monkey to take care of them. Besides, you don't have time for me, aren't you still seeing Julee?"

"Of course."

"How is that going? Are you going to get her a ring?"

Sean had to pause. The small city that Julee lived in didn't have good job prospects for Sean's kind of work. At the same time, she was a small town girl and didn't have much interest in moving to a metropolitan area.

"Long distance relationships are tough," Sean answered. "She and I need to work on geography before we work on jewelry."

"Why did things have to be so complicated?" he wondered. "When two people love each other, aren't these kinds of details supposed to work themselves out?"

It was something he had been pondering all too often lately.

Chapter 49

Sean silently fumed. He had put so much work into getting the Mustang roadworthy and now it appeared to be all for naught. The mechanic Julee had promised would look at the car bumper to bumper was not nearly as available as she had suggested.

"I can get you in mid-April," the man had commented when Sean had called to set up the appointment. "I've had a lot of interest in my bumper-to-bumper package but it was a holiday promotion and we've now found that it was wildly under-priced. I have to spread those services out so that I can reserve space for my paying customers."

Sean had purposely called several weeks in advance, feeling it would be plenty of notice. Yet, his initial plan to stop through town and get the vehicle's tune-up on his way to Nick's state tournament was now not an option. Of course, the other thing that was not an option was Sean paying to have the car tuned up locally. Where was that money going to come from?

Now his only option remaining was to drive twelve hours each way on winter roads in a vehicle which had not moved more than a few blocks under its own power in over a decade. The tournament was a full week earlier this year than last year which helped to guarantee that snow and ice would be present on the roads.

"I hope you're a better mechanic than you give yourself credit for," he muttered to himself.

Missing this tournament was just not an option.

Chapter 50

Nick looked across the table and saw Sandi fuming. He took an extra helping of meat and a scoop of mashed potatoes, all the while considering how much extra running he would need to do to burn it off.

The meal itself wasn't the issue. Nick weighed 151 at the end of practice and life would have been fine had Tanner, just returning to the line-up after two weeks, not tipped the scales at 154. Coach Nestor had gone ape and, after laying into his son about needing to cut seven pounds by the following morning, he threw his hands up in the air and said, "Forget it. You lost your spot. Castle, you're 145 tomorrow, Patron has been wrestling well at 152 so he can stay there; we'll forfeit 160."

Nick had frozen, suddenly stuck between needing to shed four pounds and needing to save face with his girlfriend and her parents who had just cooked a feast for him. He was about as nervous as he could remember being.

"Do you like duck?" Mr. Davis asked.

"It smells wonderful," Nick commented, trying to take enough to make his plate look full while at the same time ensuring that the slice was thin enough to carry minimum weight.

"Sandi's mom does an amazing job with duck," Mr. Davis continued. "It will keep you strong for your tournament tomorrow."

Nick just nodded as his girlfriend's intense stare continued. He regretted every word of his monologue from a few days earlier about how Mrs. Davis could go all out and he would enjoy every last morsel. He knew how much work must have gone into this feast and lamented that he couldn't gorge himself until he split his pants ... clearly this is what the entire Davis family would like to see. Only Sandi knew of his predicament, and she had already voiced her opinion in private that he should have told Coach Nestor to find someone else to starve himself for tomorrow.

The boy eyed the spread and felt incredibly awkward. He had never had a full French meal before. Were there truly seven courses?

Mrs. Davis changed the subject, which was a breath of fresh air.

"I understand you're going to be on the news tomorrow night."

Nick blushed a bit but smiled sheepishly.

"Yeah."

He still wasn't sure how he felt about being on camera but Sandi was quick to add her own input.

"Nick doesn't like talking in front of people, but the people at the TV station promised that he wouldn't have to say any more than his name and that he's a wrestler."

"Are you nervous, Nick?" Sandi's Dad asked.

"A little bit," Nick admitted. "But, if I can't get my name right and say 'I'm a wrestler,' I've got bigger problems than most."

The small talk continued and it felt like one of the longest evenings of Nick's life as he continued sampling the fare, worrying about the calories and lamenting that he may let Sandi and her parents and / or his teammates down.

* * *

On the far side of town Tanner was drenched in sweat.

"I've got to make 145," he thought. "Get a good sweat going, change to warm dry clothes, let the pores keep draining in bed, and don't let Castle down by making him cut in the morning."

It was a must-win tournament the next day. Being at 145 would give him his best opportunity to set himself up for winning at the conference tournament and then at state.

"Do it," he thought. "It's water weight, you only need to keep it off until after weigh-in."

Chapter 51

Nick found a nice warm place in the stands to eat a healthy snack and clear his head after weigh-in. Tanner had arrived at South the same time as Nick this morning, an hour before the bus was to depart for the hour-long eastward trek across the state border to a small tournament. The two of them had worked out feverishly and afterward, found that Tanner was within a pound of making weight while Nick was still a pound and a half high. When Coach Nestor left it to the two of them to make the call, Tanner was set on proving that he could make weight while Nick was comfortable staying at 152, meaning that Patron had cut down to 152 for nothing.

It was only mildly uncomfortable until Patron stopped over.

"Castle, can I talk to you?"

The question itself wasn't as odd as the way Patron was acting. He largely whispered the phrase to Nick who looked around suspiciously before raising his eyebrows and nodding, "yes."

"Don't look now," Patron continued under his breath, "but I think that's my dad over by the gym door."

Nick tried to be casual as he glanced over toward the entrance to see a weathered man in his forties whose long black hair could definitely have put him in the same gene pool as Patron. His tattered jacket made him easy to spot. The tournament was in a rural area at a school that was a co-op of three neighboring small towns. Nick pictured the man to be a farm hand of some sort.

"How do you know?" Nick asked. Patron had only ever mentioned his father briefly, noting that he hadn't seen him since he was five when the man's relationship with Patron's mom had ended and he had largely disappeared.

"The last picture I have with him was from not long before he left. He was wearing that same coat and his hair really hasn't changed much ... maybe it's a little shorter now."

Nick nodded again, "Could you call your mom and ask if he lives around here?"

Patron got quiet for several seconds, like he didn't know what to say.

"I haven't talked to my mom since ninth grade," he eventually volunteered. "Her boyfriend had been beating me up sometimes and one night, I flipped and went after him with a bat. I got a couple of good hits in too before my mom grabbed me and called the cops. That was the last night I lived with my mom."

Nick sat quietly. He knew that Patron had been living with foster parents but didn't realize the reason.

"I'm pretty sure it's my dad," Patron continued, "... and I was ..." the boy looked away and stopped.

Nick waited patiently for a few moments before prodding his friend to continue.

"You were ... ?"

Patron looked nervous and a bit sheepish.

"I was wondering if I could wrestle 152. I don't know that I can place at 160 and, if that is him, I'd like to at least do reasonably well."

Nick stared at the boy for a moment. While the rural tournament didn't have a line-up of the pre-Christmas tournament or other top events, he was sure there were a few individuals with solid skills in the mix. He wanted to tell his friend to push ahead at 160 but caught himself before responding.

Patron had come out for the team at Nick's request. He had wrestled 171 at the pre-Christmas tournament as Nick moved up to avoid Chester. Certainly, moving up for one little tournament was the least Nick could do to pay back his friend.

"Sure," Nick finally replied. "You've sacrificed a lot for the team this year and, I didn't tell you at the time, but you took a hit for me when you moved up at the pre-Christmas tournament ... at 152, I would have had to wrestle Troftgruben. I'll go 160, then consider us even."

Castle had to smile when he saw his buddy break out into a sheepish grin. He felt relieved to finally come clean about December.

While he didn't know exactly what he might be getting into by moving up, he was pretty sure that there was nobody here more fierce than the 160-pounders he had beaten earlier in the year. He pondered later whether or not he would have agreed to move up had he seen the bracket sheets before agreeing to let Patron have 152.

Chapter 52

Nick noticed Patron smiling. Wrestlers don't smile often during matches, but Nick's friend was letting one show during his match for third place ... a match he led 9 – 3 in the closing seconds.

The boys had noticed earlier that the awards podium had room for five. This made Nick smile as well, knowing that Patron would have a place on the podium with his father present.

Patron had braved it out and gone to talk to the man after the first round and had not left until he was called for his second match, at which point Patron reported to Nick that his dad had learned that he was wrestling via box scores in the newspaper. As the man didn't have a vehicle, he had walked five miles that morning in the cold and snow to make it to this tournament, knowing that it may very well be his only opportunity to see the boy in action.

Nick had wished that Patron could have won that next match but getting called for clasping again had cost him a point which became the difference in the match, requiring him to win his third match to get to the consolation final.

Nick's own day had gone as expected for a wrestler of his caliber. Even wrestling up a weight class, he had still pinned his first opponent and then won by major decision in the semi-finals. He learned that his opponent in the finals was ranked high in this neighboring state but pushed that from his mind right now. It was shaping up to be a great day. Patron was about to earn a spot on the awards stand in front of his father, and Nick would get home just in time to make it to the TV station and smile for the camera while being honored as a top athlete in the city and area. Why wouldn't a person smile?

Chapter 53

The sting of the mat hurt far less than the words that accompanied it.

"Two points green," the ref bellowed.

Nick didn't need to see the scoreboard. He knew that the score was now 3 – 3 and that he needed to escape to avoid overtime.

It wasn't that he had underestimated his opponent; Nick had perhaps come out overly cautious in the first period. It had taken him well over a minute to score his first takedown but his seasoned competitor had escaped before the period had ended.

In the second, Nick had chosen down and quickly found that riding was one of his opponent's specialties. The boy had kept his full weight on top of Nick for the entire period, forcing Castle to use a lot of energy in trying to retain his base and work upward. Due to his opponent's seemingly indifferent attitude toward turning Nick, the boy had been repeatedly cautioned for stalling, eventually helping Nick earn a single penalty point to go up 3 – 1.

Nick entered the third period feeling about as tired as he could remember. Whether this was due to his opponent's second period riding strategy or not wasn't clear. What was clear was that his requirement to cut a bunch of weight followed by the choice to wrestle up put him in a bad place. The other boy had chosen "neutral" in the third, which on any other day would have been to Castle's advantage. Yet, this day, he felt completely drained.

His rival secured a takedown and then a chicken wing with twenty seconds left and all Nick could do was scramble to avoid being turned and look for ways to return to his base or find the edge of the mat. His efforts were enough to end regulation with the tie.

Moving to overtime, neither wrestler had been able to score in the first period but Nick had chosen bottom position in the second and gotten an escape for a renewed lead.

As Nick began the third period on top, contemplating how he could possibly survive an ultimate tie-breaker should his opponent escape, some crowd noise seeped past his defenses. He was wrestling the local favorite and the crowd's verbose applause reflected that, pulling even more energy from the exhausted South wrestler.

Pushing everything external from his mind, Nick focused on staying on top, feeling that the best way to do so would be to ride legs. Tragically, he could not get his long legs in deep enough.

"You're too high," Coach Nestor warned as Nick frantically did everything possible to keep his opponent in his control.

Wrestling is a sport of instants. Escapes and pins require less than a second to come to fruition. In this match, nearly 25 seconds of battling for position came to an end with the other wrestler shaking Nick off balance, coming back around for the reversal and securing Castle in his iron grip. In that same instant, Nick's undefeated record came to an end.

Chapter 54

Tanner sat in the front of the bus, near his dad, beaming with pride. He had just taken a large step. Sure it was a small tournament but he had won the championship. His extra efforts to make weight had paid off. He felt a twinge of guilt due to how things had panned out for Nick. With Castle taking second, had the torch been passed? Whether it was just for an evening or the start of something permanent, this was Tanner's night and he spent the ride silently soaking it in.

* * *

The two wrestlers sat together toward the back of the bus, not saying a word. Both sat with sweatshirt hoods up and eyes closed, lost in their own little worlds.

An atypical grin of satisfaction crossed Patron's face as he listened to music, his headphones hidden somewhere under his hood. One could imagine that accomplishing his top showing of the season in front of his father had given Patron a new sense of inner peace which may supplant his day-to-day uncertainty for some time.

Next to him sat Nick in an opposite state of emotion. Still reeling from his loss, he soon realized that the awards ceremony would not be until after the heavyweight match. When he heard rumblings in the locker room that he would not show up to accept his silver medal, his sense of honor combined with a deep longing to see Patron get time on the podium prompted Nick to insist to Coach Nestor that the team stay for the ceremony.

Of course, this put the bus at risk of not making it home in time for Nick to get to his TV news event. A day later, he would regret this even more as Sandi would lament having told all of her friends and family to watch Nick on the news.

He was pretty sure that things could not get any worse. Life would only take about a week to prove him wrong ...

Chapter 55

Nick watched Sandi as she crossed the room.

She was disappointed – again – and he was of course the reason.

"I told all of my friends and family that you would be on the news last night," she started. "Most of them recorded it ... and you didn't show up. Didn't you want to be on TV?"

Nick felt empty. When he said he was fine staying for the awards ceremony, he knew there was a chance that the bus wouldn't make it back in time for the news. He figured, if it didn't, it would be disappointing to him but at least Patron would get his time on the awards stand. He never considered that Sandi and others would be expecting him to be there.

To follow-up Friday's dinner debacle with this snafu was really poor timing.

Chewie wasn't supposed to be inside the Castle house, especially not in the living room, but with both of his parents gone on Sunday afternoon, Nick had let the dog in. The animal seemed to sense that something wasn't right and parked himself on the couch beside Sandi the moment she sat down.

"We got back late," was really all Nick could muster.

The two sat there in an uncomfortable silence for what seemed like an hour. She at least had a dog to pet while Nick sat awkwardly on his own.

He pondered how they had gotten to this point in their relationship. Things had started out so well, but recently cracks had begun to surface more and more often. He felt edgy, just trying to keep things afloat.

"I'll be at opening night for your show on Thursday," Nick finally offered, filling the gap.

"That's ok," she mumbled, not even looking at him. "You don't have to. I know you don't like coming over to Riverside."

Nick seized the opportunity to cross to her couch and put his hand on her shoulder.

"You'll be amazing," he said. "I wouldn't miss it for anything."

She shook her head a bit.

"Well, if something comes up, you know I'll understand."

Nick couldn't tell whether she was inferring that she was expecting to be let down again or if she was suggesting that she didn't want him at the performance.

"He likes you a lot," Nick said, watching the way the dog snuggled close to the girl.

"What?" she asked, suddenly even more agitated.

"Chewie really feels comfortable with you. He isn't that way with everyone. He used to growl under his breath at one of Ron's girlfriends."

He leaned down to kiss her but she leaned down and kissed Chewie on the muzzle. Nick thought back to Ron chiding him about kissing the dog and how no girl would want to kiss him after he would do such a thing.

It didn't stop him from leaning down a second time, but the girl only offered her cheek.

"Dogs are just big furry lumps of love sent from God," she commented.

While Nick was quick to agree, he really wished that there was more he could do to get the relationship back on track.

Chapter 56

Everyone in the meeting looked at Sean. In most cases he was fine being the center of attention, but the tone of this meeting started out poorly and got worse.

"You're all here for the dog-and-pony show before we present it to the board of directors," one of the executives had commented to start the meeting. "Let's start with the dog."

Sean cringed when the man then put up a slide with the Roadrunner logo. He then cringed a second time when the man changed to a slide which showed financial performance versus plan. Costs were well above plan and showed up in bright red. Revenues were well below plan and the huge gap was shown in red as well.

Everyone in the room had a title of Vice President or higher except Sean who was a lowly manager. He had asked his supervisor to join him for the meeting, feeling it best to have someone to back him up as he talked through the true status of the product, but the man was inexplicably absent.

Sean fought off the cost overruns accusations, the only area which he could control in any way, by explaining that the pilot customer insisted on adding features.

"If you're going to add features," he asserted, "you have to pay for them by adding cost, adding time, or both. Nobody was willing to tell the customer that we couldn't deliver their requests, so my team and I ended up picking up the slack. Except for Christmas, nobody was able to take a day off in December, including weekends. We delivered the product and it works."

"But it doesn't work well," one of the executives shot back. "We've got dozens of customers lined up to buy these things, but everything hinges on a glowing review from the pilot customer. It's been a month and I'm not hearing anything glowing. All I hear about are the features that haven't been added."

Sean focused on staying calm as he replied.

"Yes, we received a list last week of 150 more features and changes they would like made. Only four have been on a previous list at any point. We told them that, if they wanted the product in the next year, they would have to forego half of those until a later phase. We're in phase two of development now but the product isn't going to be ready over night."

"My team can't sell an incomplete product!" the VP of Sales yelled. "You saddled us with a $35 million sales goal for the year and, during January, we were able to sell less than $0.5 million worth of product. If my people don't have a product to sell, they are going to leave and go sell our competitors' products. We spent $100 million buying a company to give us this innovative product and what was delivered looks like something from the discount bin at Wal-Mart."

Sean bristled at both the mention of the unreasonable numbers and the belittling of his team's work. Yet, he secretly had to agree that the company's purchase price had been unduly inflated. He had met his former mentor, Larry Darkins, for lunch a week earlier and the man had confided in him that, prior to being acquired, the smaller company's owners and managers had put together sales estimates five to ten times what they ever realistically expected to sell complete with bogus market assumptions to back the numbers. Contrary to rumors of Larry being fired, the man had actually resigned just before the acquisition closed in order to not profit from the inflated sales price.

"Lawyers and others will catch up with those guys someday," Larry had commented about his former peers and bosses. "I would have gotten $0.5 million in the sale but chose to walk away to avoid the trouble."

Of course, Sean didn't need additional trouble either but was currently sitting right in the middle of it.

With all eyes focused on him, he reiterated, "We can add the features. That was already the intent. My guys tell me it will take an extra six months to a year to add all of them, but it can be done."

"Six months to a year?" the VP of Marketing clarified.

"Yes."

"You should be fired," the VP continued.

"You can do that," Sean replied. "But then, the timeline changes to an extra eighteen months."

"You are excused, Sean," the Business Unit President commented.

As MacCallister assembled his materials, he hoped that the man was only referring to him being excused to leave the meeting.

Chapter 57

Flanked by Tanner and Patron, Nick sat quietly in the dark theater watching *The Glass Menagerie*.

He had fidgeted through most of the first act, feeling very uncomfortable at his old high school with all of the history and memories of emotional swings the building held.

It didn't help that Oscar was also in attendance, sitting with Tim Parks, Todd Johnson and some other Riverside thug that Nick couldn't name. Concerns about an inter-school rumble during intermission were calmed when Principal Skinner had come over to speak with the South trio between acts. Nick had to admit that he was beginning to warm up to the man who seemed resigned to the fact that it was too late for Nick to return and wrestle but not too late for the boy to continue to be an ambassador for wrestling and good sportsmanship for young athletes on the city's north side.

All in all, with the Riverside principal in the way, the thugs had done little more than cast dirty looks at Nick and his teammates. Oscar and Tim had added a few hand gestures to further relay their feelings while Skinner's back was to them but Nick simply brushed them off.

Sandi, of course, been amazing through the entire show. Her character was self-conscious and walked with a slight limp due to one leg being slightly shorter than the other. Sandi pulled it off wonderfully as the limp was very subtle rather than over-exaggerated. In many ways, Nick felt like he was able to connect with her character on multiple levels. Her personality was so much like his own and, of course, she was being played by his girlfriend. The boy just wanted to run up on stage and give her a big squeeze as he managed to focus on the show, leaving all angst about Oscar and company behind.

Sadly, his break from anxiety was short-lived as the second act wore on. Aiden had emerged as a gentleman caller. Sandi's character, Laura, had been interested in him during her high school years. Nick cringed when the two began dancing.

"Don't touch my girlfriend," he thought, glaring at the boy but knowing that the two were bound to do whatever the script called for.

Then, after what seemed like an eternity, the dancing stopped when the two bumped into a table and broke Laura's glass unicorn.

Nick was silently relieved. The unicorn was Laura's favorite possession; hopefully, she would kick him out so Nick no longer had to look at the well-groomed boy ... but that was not meant to be.

A few minutes later, after a long string of dialogue about self-confidence, Aiden seemed to be moving in.

"Somebody ought to, ought to kiss you, Laura."

Nick's chest tightened and reflexes caused him to grip the armrests of his chair. He looked on in horror as Aiden kissed Sandi, Nick's Sandi, in front of a sold-out theater.

"Castle, he's kissing your woman!" Oscar yelled, loud enough for the entire crowd to hear.

The actors didn't seem to notice, but Nick absorbed the comment without so much as a glance in Oscar's direction, all the while his knuckles getting white as they gripped the armrest.

The rest of the show didn't register to Nick. For all he knew, it could have ended with space aliens or a nuclear attack. All he could see as he sat in the audience was his girlfriend kissing some other guy.

Chapter 58

The Mustang growled lightly as it made its way down the highway. The serene rhythmic thumping of the tires over pavement did little to calm Sean's nerves.

It was a day that had started differently than most. Sean had passed on taking the train to work in order to drive his Mustang. He had finally gotten all of the crucial driving functions operational so today would be the first minor road test of the classic vehicle – preparation for its pending interstate trip, less than a week away.

Further, it would ensure that he had transportation home in case his work happy hour ran too late for the final train. As an added bonus, he might be able to earn back some points by serving as designated driver for a drunk co-worker.

He really needed some kind, ANY kind, of good fortune right now. After the recent executive meeting in preparation for the board meeting, a lot of angry looks were being thrown his way. Nobody seemed to care about unreasonable expectations or burned out employees. Bonus pay-outs were on the line, which meant that the entire upper echelon at the company was going to lose out if he and his team didn't provide a miracle and, quite likely, based on each customer's unique wants, even if they did.

The road test gave him confidence as the tattered car performed like a champion. He was sure that any state patrol officer he passed would question the vehicle's ability to operate safely. Yet, what the car currently lacked in looks, it seemed to make up for in stability as it chugged along just above the speed limit with plenty of pedal left for passing.

While the car lacked looks, nothing could be further from the truth for Sean's passenger. As the happy hour ran late, extending past 9:00, Jeremy had gotten inebriated and began overtly hitting on Enid. Sean had been looking for a graceful way to exit before the group changed venues for a house party, and Enid had turned to him for a ride home.

His agreeing to her request left the two truly alone together for the first time. She was wearing red and looked absolutely fabulous. His mind wandered and he tried to assure himself that it was chivalry that drove his actions and not hormones.

The twenty-minute drive was filled with small talk driven mainly by her asking questions about him.

"How long have you been with the company?" she asked him.

"Almost a year," he replied.

"Where were you before that?"

"College."

"What? You mean grad school?"

"No, just my bachelor's degree in engineering."

She was silent for a few moments.

"So, you're twenty-three?"

"Yes."

"And you're in charge of a $35 million project?"

"Yes," he replied again, resisting the urge to tell her what he had learned from Larry.

He glanced over at her and noticed that she was looking at the door. The door panel was missing and in disarray, much like the rest of the car's interior.

"I'm sorry about the condition of the car," he apologized. "It will look much better when I'm done restoring it."

"It's ok," she replied, "I don't look so great tonight either."

"You look amazing," he said, before he could stop himself.

"Flattery will get you everywhere," she noted, causing his blood pressure to shoot through the roof.

He only smiled in response.

"Nothing is going to happen," he told himself as he clutched the steering wheel a bit tighter. "I've got a girlfriend and I don't want anything to happen."

He glanced over at her.

"Who do you think you're kidding?" he thought. "Of course I want something to happen. I want everything to happen. I just need to get her out of my car and drive away so that nothing does happen."

He pulled into the lot of her condominium. Sean had no idea how much money Enid made but figured she must be doing ok from the looks of her home.

"Thanks for the ride, Sean, I really appreciate it."

"It was really no problem at all. I needed to get going anyway and it gave me a chance to put a few more test miles on my beautiful car," he said, trying to keep things light.

"The real beauty is on the inside," she said, looking at him and sending another jolt up his spine. "Do you mind walking me upstairs?"

He suddenly felt light-headed.

"There is this guy ..." she continued, "... and I'd feel a lot safer if you could take me up to my apartment."

Sean was really getting flustered. Surely she couldn't be hitting on him, yet the way she looked at him when she had said that the beauty is on the inside made him feel she might be interested. Was he reading the signs correctly or just flattering himself?

"I can do that," his mouth said before his brain could stop it.

They got out of the car and made their way up the sidewalk to the door. As she got them through the security door, he thought about how the building seemed completely safe and that she had nothing to truly worry about.

"She's interested in me," he thought. "What do I do? I can't cheat on Julee. Even if that isn't meant to last, I can't let it end with me hooking up with someone else."

He tried to justify bringing her upstairs as they reached the second floor landing and began ascending one more flight. She smelled so good and looked impeccable. She had always been so wonderful to him, why would he not see if something could work with her? Maybe they would have to keep things secret seeing as they worked together. But she was there, living in the same city as him. He could see her every day. They could go to lunch and do things together every night after work ... not just on occasional weekends which found them both so tired that they settled for each other's leftovers.

If she invited him into her apartment and he declined, would that be the end of this? Would it cause problems for them at work? He felt like he was on the brink of losing his job already; would this push him into the unemployment line? Then, what would Julee say? Would she ask him why he got fired, and would he have to tell her about how he took a woman who was beyond gorgeous up to her apartment?

His heart was racing and his mind spinning but he made himself one promise, "Nothing will happen tonight. I will break up with Julee when she visits this weekend if it is clear that Enid is the right woman for me, but I won't cheat on my girlfriend."

The third floor landing seemed to spin as he opened the door to usher her into the third floor hallway.

... and from there, the night got complicated.

Chapter 59

The three South wrestlers stood in the Riverside hallway, not saying a word.

Tanner watched the crowd with a snide look on his face while Patron mainly stared at the ground, shuffling a bit to the left and the right. Nick stood motionless, silently fuming.

"Let's get out of here," Tanner stated but shut up after an angry glance from Nick.

Nick would stand there and wait for Sandi, really not having any idea what he would say when she finally arrived.

"We just practice for the play," she had commented over a month earlier. Had Nick had any idea about the kissing scene, he would have inquired further at the time. Now it was too late. She had kissed that preppy kid in front of Nick and hundreds of others. Nick tried to shake the memory from his mind but knew it wouldn't fade anytime soon. Who knows what the kid would have tried in solitude with the girl.

"I trust my girlfriend, I trust my girlfriend, I trust my girlfriend ..." Nick began repeating to himself, all the while feeling angst in the back of his mind.

Why hadn't she told him about this scene? Is this why she had been acting so odd this last month and had gone so far as to suggest that he didn't need to come to the show?

To the onlooker, Nick probably looked non-threatening. He just stood, rigid as a statue, but inside he felt like his heart might explode and he really needed to throttle someone – preferably the preppy kid but how would Sandi respond to that? It didn't matter anyway. He couldn't risk getting in a fight right now and getting suspended from wrestling as he had a year earlier. Whether you're a willing participant or not, fighting was grounds for suspension. The conference tournament was the following day and state was in a week. There was too much at stake.

A police officer walked by, eyeing the three wrestlers suspiciously but saying nothing. Nick wondered if his thoughts could get him arrested for assault.

His fists clenched reflexively as Oscar appeared around the corner with Tim Parks and the other cretin in tow. Todd Johnson was suspiciously absent from the group, which seemed to be looking for the South wrestlers. They looked like a ragged group of gunslingers out of an old western movie as they strode down the corridor toward Nick and his friends.

"I told you she was cheatin' on you, Castle," Oscar called out as a half-full hallway of onlookers turned their attention toward the six boys.

Nick just glared at his former friend until the boys were within a few feet of each other.

"I trust my girlfriend," he announced, really not knowing what else to say.

Tim immediately got in Nick's face, close enough so Nick could smell the stale smoke on the boy's breath, clothes and hair. Tim's scruffy friend stood only inches behind him, looking like he was ready for some action. Todd Johnson's bulky frame finally appeared around the corner, twenty yards away but lumbering in the direction of the confrontation.

"Let's go, Castle," Tim taunted. "You think you're pretty tough when you can hide on the wrestling mat but I'm going to kick your face in right here in the hall."

In the brief moment of indecision, Nick pondered whether flattening this kid and alleviating some pent-up frustration would be worth possibly getting kicked off the wrestling team. That moment was all it took for him to lose his chance as Patron leapt forward and, in two steps, drove Tim sideways and slammed him into a row of lockers.

Tim was able to stay on his feet while Patron punched him twice, knocking the wind out of him, and then slammed the back of the boy's head into the locker. The other scruffy thug took a step toward the scuffle but, to Nick's surprise, Todd Johnson grabbed the kid, who then turned to glare at Nick. Todd abruptly smacked him in the back of the head.

"Don't be stupid," Todd told his friend. "Look what happens to stupid people," he continued, pointing to Tim who was now crumpled on the floor with Patron kicking him.

The whole commotion lasted less than ten seconds before the police officer returned and broke things up.

Nick stepped in to pull Patron off of Tim and only then noticed Tanner and Oscar standing toe-to-toe, glaring at each other.

"What happened here?" the officer asked.

"Those guys just attacked my friends," Oscar yelled, pointing at Patron and Nick.

Several spectators from the hallway chimed in, some refuting and others verifying Oscar's story. The crowd continued to grow and Principal Skinner re-emerged and talked with the officer.

"These are the two I saw fighting," the officer commented to Skinner, pointing at Patron and Tim. "I'm going to need to take them downtown."

Nick didn't know what to say to protect his friend who had just potentially saved his wrestling career.

"Mr. Skinner," he finally commented, drawing a slightly irritated look from the man. "Those two were getting in my face. Patron just stepped in to help me."

"Did you hit anyone?" the Principal asked Nick.

"No."

"Did he hit anyone?" the Principal pointed to Patron.

"Yes," Patron answered before Nick could say anything.

"I'm sorry, son. You're going to have to accompany the officer downtown to sort this out," Skinner said to Patron. "Nick, I'll escort you and your other friend to the door to keep you out of trouble."

"I'll get you Saturday," Tanner growled to Oscar as he began following Nick and the principal.

"I'm going to tear both of your shoulders out this time," Oscar replied.

The stage was set for another confrontation at the conference tournament.

Chapter 60

As he sat in the jail cell, waiting to make bail, Sean couldn't help but be agitated by the night's events.

How it had all happened was a bit of a blur. He remembered walking into the third floor hallway with Enid and immediately being yelled at. He had turned to see a man hastily walking toward them and calling both of them a variety of colorful, inappropriate and disgusting names.

Sean immediately took a defensive stance and inserted himself between Enid and this angry individual only to initially be shoved aside. He quickly regained his balance and tackled the man before he could get to Enid who started yelling, "Don't hurt him."

Neighbors emerged from their condos as Sean and the man scuffled on the floor, throwing punches and drawing blood before the neighbors were able to tear them apart. The blood was predominantly from the other man, and a variety of people stepped in to separate the two. Someone called the police who arrived quickly.

While being held against the wall by three condo owners, Sean pieced together that this man who attacked him was Enid's husband and was apparently named Gary. The news about her having a husband came as a surprise to Sean as Enid had never worn a ring or mentioned anything about being married.

The story of the woman who was the first to peek out of her condo was that she had seen Sean tackle Gary. Others who chimed in had seen Sean getting the better of the man and it all led to him being brought downtown to face possible assault charges.

Thus, he sat in the cell, examining a deep rug burn on his right forearm, which was bleeding, and cleaning it out with a damp paper towel while he considered why Enid would invite him up to her apartment to meet her vicious husband.

"No good deed goes un-punished," he thought as he mulled over the situation.

In the morning, he would make bail and be sent home. Julee should be there by the time he arrived and would likely wonder where on earth he was. Sometimes bad choices make good stories when a person lives to tell about the experience. It would certainly be an interesting story to tell but he questioned how she might react. Their relationship had been stretched recently by distance and questions about whether they would land in a common area in the future. Would a night in jail after escorting a beautiful woman to her apartment be the last straw?

He would likely see Julee around 10:00 a.m. Until then, he had several hours to think.

Chapter 61

Nick was in his best mood of the past week as he waited for the rest of the team to arrive in the second van. The conference tournament could not have gone better for him personally as he marched through round after round, repeating as a conference champion. This success partially improved his mood with the theater surprise from the prior night still weighing on him.

It would be the last event of the season which would require the team to take multiple vehicles. While all wrestlers on the team had wrestled up to or beyond their seedings, only three made it to the state tournament – only slightly better than Riverside's two.

Tanner had borrowed extra clothing from Nick for cutting weight early that morning and had been the first South wrestler to gain a state tournament berth this season. The boy made good on his threat from the previous evening and toppled Oscar in the 145-pound conference championship. Then, after Nick's 152-pound championship, Seagull surprised everyone with a third-place finish at 215 to make it a trio.

Sadly, Patron's third-place finish a week earlier would be both his finest moment and his final match. His run-in at Riverside after Sandi's show disqualified him from the conference tournament due to the school's strict stance on off-mat altercations for its athletes. In the back of his mind, Nick suspected that he had been the true target and that the entire clash had been designed to get him suspended from the team before state.

He had made himself a promise earlier that he would go out of his way to thank Patron for stepping in for him. But now, his main thought was that he needed to get his leather mittens back from Tanner before heading home. With temperatures hovering in the single digits, he would need them for his Sunday run.

The headlights entering the parking lot revealed themselves to be those of the second van and Nick jumped from the first van to go meet his friends.

All smiles upon seeing Seagull in the front passenger seat, Nick pulled the passenger door open and congratulated his big friend again as soon as the van rolled to a halt.

"You're on your way, big man," he commented jovially, shaking the quiet giant's shoulders. "Your instincts in the consolation finals paid off."

Nick then grabbed the separator between the passenger door and the sliding door with his right hand as he steadied himself and peered into the van's back section.

"Tanner, do you have my choppers?"

"I've got them and your t-shirt and sweatshirt, which are soaked in sweat and seem to be frozen after sitting all day in the back of the van."

"Wash those shirts before you return them," Nick said with a big smile. "I just need the mittens for now."

Nick's toothy grin suddenly turned to one of shock and agony as he felt a searing pain shoot through his right hand and he let out a scream.

It took him about half an instance to realize that Seagull, unaware that Nick was holding onto the separator between the doors, had slammed the passenger door shut, crushing Nick's fingers in so-doing.

The larger boy quickly reopened the door, but the damage was done as blood dripped down the door jam from the mangled digits.

"Let's get you over to the ER," Coach Nestor urged as the other boys rallied around getting their star some medical attention.

Chapter 62

Nick winced and continued looking away as the doctor continued to examine his fingers. The boy had taken a look at the bloody, crushed digits earlier and gotten nauseated – uncommon for a kid who had seen his share of blood.

The doctor shook his head before addressing both Nick and his father. How many times had this man had to treat Nick's and Ron's injuries and ailments over the years? Nick had seen this same disappointed look on the doctor's face more times than he could remember. The boy became uneasy and slightly agitated as he waited for the assessment and what it would mean to Nick's final push toward state.

"The pinkie and index finger will be largely all right. You sliced the tips off of them but didn't quite get the bone so, while they will continue to bleed for several days before the skin coverage grows back, you won't need to worry much about them.

"Unfortunately, the middle and ring finger weren't so lucky. You shattered the distal phalanx on both of them. We're going to have to take out some bone fragments and try to clean those up the best we can before splinting them. They will be tender for a while. The nails will fall off in a day or two but they'll grow back."

"What do I do about them during practice?" Nick asked and watched the doctor's expression change from one of disappointment to one of irritation.

"No practice," the physician responded. "Rest them. Let them heal for the next ten days. The shattered bones will need splints to keep them straight so that they heal correctly."

Nick's temper began to rise, "The state tournament starts Friday ..."

"... and if you choose to wrestle in it, those fingers will become a painful, mangled mess," the doctor interrupted, inflaming Nick's anger.

"Can you cut them off?"

"What??!!!!" the doctor and Mr. Castle both shouted in unison.

"If you cut off those bad bones in the tips, will the fingers heal faster?"

"We're talking about your hand, the rest of your life ..."

"We're talking about the STATE TOURNAMENT next week and I've got to train for it!"

"You're just like your brother," the doctor scolded.

"I'm NOT like my brother!" Nick shot back, but bit his lip instead of voicing the rest of his thought. Tears of anger and frustration welled in his eyes as he stared sternly at the two men, keeping those final words inside.

"... my brother is a state champion."

The room was silent. Significant choices had to be made.

Chapter 63

Quietly, Sean worked on breakfast. It would be a feast consisting of omelets, bacon, fresh strawberries, and his famous banana pancakes made from his grandma's recipe. It was a lot of work, but Julee was worth it, even if she probably wouldn't eat much.

He was up early Sunday morning despite having been up talking with Julee until sometime between three and four a.m. Communication was what their relationship had needed and communication was what it got.

Sean had laid out the whole Friday night story early on Saturday.

"Is she pretty?" had been Julee's first question regarding Enid.

"Yes," Sean had admitted, "very."

But from there, she relayed no hint of suspicion about his motives or intentions. What would have happened had Gary not been there would never be known, but deep down Sean still believed that he would have done the honorable thing.

The topic of their own relationship and its current hardships then took center stage. Neither blamed the other for anything. They were in a tough spot, being held apart by careers, geographical preferences and so many unknowns. Yet, over the course of several hours, they dug to the root issues. She didn't want to move to the heart of the city, which was where he worked. He couldn't find a similar job in a community the size of hers. But if they were to live in the far northern suburbs, he would still be able to commute by a very long train ride, and she would likely be able to find a teaching job while being far enough from the city to still feel comfortable.

She nervously told him that, if they did get married someday, she wouldn't want to change her name. It surprised him that she seemed to think this would be an issue for him, but truly it had never crossed his mind that she would want to take his name.

"Ms. Novak," he said. "I want you to keep your own name for the rest of your life."

They candidly discussed finances, first loves, religion, childhood quirks, family illnesses and their deepest fears. No topic was off limits and, by the time they realized that 3:00 a.m. had come and gone, they had never felt closer.

Now, several hours later, Sean separated wilted spinach into a pile for himself while carefully drying the freshest pieces for Julee's omelet. In his mind, spinach had no place in an omelet but, like so many things she had suggested in the past 24 hours, he was willing to give it a try. He poured the eggs into the skillet and hummed softly and happily as he cooked.

Chapter 64

Nick sat in the living room. His whole body was shaking as he wondered what kind of cosmic landmine he could have possibly stepped on to generate such a landslide of bad luck. His fingers hurt, the splints were annoying, and the bleeding was only contained by keeping pressure on them.

Yet, the injured fingers were not the main source of the boy's consternation. The phone had rung just before church and Nick had unfortunately been the one to answer it, only to get an earful from the angry caller.

"WHAT DO YOU THINK YOU'RE DOING, CASTLE?!!!!" the tirade began.

The hair on the back of Nick's neck had bristled as he went into his defensive mode, both trying to fend off the verbal attack and figure out who his assailant was.

"152 is MY weight class, CASTLE. MINE!!!"

Sheer terror joined the anger Nick was already feeling as he suddenly recognized the voice. It was Chester Troftgruben's.

"Chester?"

"WHAT ARE YOU TRYING TO PROVE, CASTLE?"

"I ..."

"YOU CAN'T BEAT ME!"

"But I thought ..."

"I CAN'T BELIEVE YOU! I'M GOING TO CRUSH YOU LIKE THE INSECT YOU ARE!"

"Ches ..."

The line went dead and Nick was left to agonize over the conversation as he quickly checked the western conference results. He cringed as he found that Chester had decisively won the 152-pound title.

"How could I have been so stupid?" he asked himself over and over again through church and lunch. A day earlier, it had seemed that Tanner making it to state at 145 and Nick at 152 gave them two legitimate contenders for state titles. Yet, with Tanner's shoulder still a bit tender, Nick's finger injury and now this news about Chester, it looked like South's dry spell would likely continue.

By early afternoon, his only salvation was his visit from Sandi. She had been so distant lately, but today there was no wrestling, no theater and, with Nick's parents out for the afternoon, no other people to interfere with them. It would simply be Sandi and Nick – alone together. He hoped to talk about the theater situation with her and find a way to ease his mind about the future of their relationship.

He heard Chewie barking and knew that the girl was getting near. He sprinted to the door and watched as the overly-friendly dog got dangerously close to the moving car as it pulled into the driveway. Sandi wasted no time disembarking and petting the happy animal as she power-walked toward the house.

Nick opened the door and grabbed her in a bear hug, lifting her off her feet, turning his body, and setting her down inside the entry way. He moved in for a kiss, but oddly, she turned her head, only offering her cheek which he readily planted one on.

The dog whimpering on the steps distracted him for a moment while Sandi took off her boots.

"Good boy," Nick said, patting the dog on its head and tousling its ears. "You're my good boy," he remarked before shutting the door and shaking off the bitter cold.

"He's going to get himself killed if he keeps chasing cars like that," Sandi commented, taking off her coat – Nick's letterman's jacket – and hanging it on a hook in the entryway. It didn't seem odd to Nick at the time that she was wearing a lighter jacket underneath in addition to a sweater and who knows how many additional layers beneath that.

There was something about her eyes. They were a bit more distant than even in recent weeks, and it gave Nick pause.

Avoiding eye contact, she turned and walked into the living room and started her story even before she sat down on the couch.

"I got in to the Sorbonne, Nick. I'm not staying here next year for school."

He wasn't surprised but his emotions ranged from disappointed to proud. He did his best to convey the latter as he congratulated her.

"Congratulations, that's great ..."

"It is great," she broke in, still not looking him in the eye, "but it means that next year, we will see each other far less than this year. I can't ..."

She trailed off to silence as a sizable lump formed in Nick's stomach. He needed to say something, anything.

"We'll make it work."

"Nick, no ..." she trailed off again.

He looked at her eyes again. Those same eyes had sparkled not so long ago but now looked hazy as they focused, not on Nick's face, but on his taped fingers.

"Do they hurt?" she asked softly, changing the subject.

"They'll be fine," he replied in a matching tone.

"Your mom said they're mangled."

It was just like his mom to worry too much and pass that on to Sandi.

"My mom hasn't even seen them. Only two are broken," he replied, "the others just lost some skin. They'll all be fine before we know it."

She looked at Nick's fingers. Even with the layers of gauze and bandages, the dried blood still showed through.

"So you've got broken fingers and you're going to the state tournament. To prove what?!!!"

"I'm not proving anything. I'm going to win the state title."

"Nick, before Christmas that boy hurt you so bad that you couldn't move for a week. Now you're saying that you can go win when you can't even use your hand. Are you insane?"

Nick reeled for a moment, like he had just been kicked.

"You're going to end up with some serious, life-altering injury. And for what? So you can prove that you're as good as your brother?"

"Ron has nothing to do with this. I'm going to win the state title. It's what I've been working toward since elementary school. A week from now, it will be over. I won't get another chance."

He sat there staring at her for a moment.

"… and I'm not going to get injured. I'll wrestle through this, protect my hand, win my championship and be just fine. Besides, there are rules that prevent serious injuries in wrestling. Life-altering injuries have been all but eliminated," he said, not knowing how incorrect this statement would be a week later.

"Just trust me. I know what I'm capable of. I have to wrestle, Sandi."

"You don't HAVE TO wrestle!" The irritation was bordering on anger. Nick opened his mouth but didn't get to speak before the girl abruptly stood up and walked toward the door.

"I'm not going to get hurt." He tried to take her hand with his left hand but she pulled it away. "I'm going to win the state title and I want you there with me."

Given this morning's conversation with Chester, he didn't even believe this to be true but he had to tell her in hopes of spurring his own confidence.

"I can't watch you ruin yourself this way, Nick."

"It's one more tournament. The STATE tournament."

His heart was racing as she got to the doorway and didn't look back.

"Goodbye, Nick."

He grabbed the letterman's jacket and tried to give it to her as she pushed the door open.

"No!" She pushed it away and fled into the cold.

He ran out the door after her, pain filling his chest as he watched her race to her car, jump in, put it into gear and drive away.

Chewie seemed to sense that something was wrong and joined Nick on the front steps. As Sandi raced away, a cloud of dust kicked up from the gravel driveway. The dog sensed the boy's pain, pushed his nose into Nick's leg and let out a small whimper.

Nick sat down and hugged the dog, seeing the dust dissipate as the car grew smaller and smaller in the distance.

"You're all I've got now, Bud," the boy whispered, feeling only emptiness and sorrow. Valentine's Day was looming and it appeared that he would be spending both the holiday and likely the rest of his life alone.

The freezing temperatures and bitter wind were not enough to keep the two from staying in that same spot for a long time.

Chapter 65

Nick arrived at the high school. Austin, the custodian, greeted him at the door.

"Working out again, Nick?" the man asked.

Nick just nodded in reply. By his best estimate, he had slept fewer than three hours the prior night as he tossed and turned, his mind spinning about Sandi. Words didn't come easily on his best days so they would be non-existent this morning. At 2:00 a.m. he had thought of plenty of brilliant things to say to Sandi to win her back, but it wasn't the right time to call her house. By morning, all of the notes he had scrawled just seemed like gibberish.

There was so much going through his mind. He wondered how his whole world had changed in the past 36 hours. He had suddenly lost his girlfriend and his hope of winning a state title all at once. He trudged down the hall thinking less about working out than about how to get his head on straight.

Defeat is an awkward thing. He had gotten his hopes up so high in all areas of life and his confidence had accompanied them. At the start of the season, he was sure that he would win the state title, go to college on a scholarship, marry Sandi, and everything else in his life would continue to work out. The events of the past few days not only quashed that view of how his life would end up but, in doing so, tainted everything else he saw as well. Over the course of the season, the South wrestling room had taken on a feeling of "home," but this morning it had transformed back into a dank and cold cinder-block room reeking of stale sweat.

He looked at his fingers and confirmed that his options were limited. The tips continued to bleed whenever he removed or loosened the bandages and gauze. Constant pressure seemed to be the only remedy, even when he was resting, so he assumed that running and really getting his blood pumping would result in making them spew blood all over. Live wrestling was certainly out as he needed to let them heal as much as possible if there were any chance of him competing at state.

"You made it."

Nick jumped at the sound of the voice. He knew that Tanner wasn't going to make it to practice and assumed that he'd have the room to himself. He was shocked to see Patron, of all people, walking into the room.

"Hey, Bud," Nick called out with a tired smile. "What are you doing here?"

"Just a glutton for punishment like you," his friend replied. "I heard Seagull smashed your fingers."

Nick held his hand in the air to display the bandaged mess.

"But you're still going to wrestle?"

Nick huffed and chuckled a bit under his breath.

"My doctor says I shouldn't and Sandi doesn't want me to."

"What about your parents?"

"My dad told me last night that he'll leave it up to me. But I get the feeling that he's worried. Am I stupid to go into the most important tournament of the year with fingers looking like this?"

"You've got a charmed life, Castle. At least you're in the state tournament."

"Yeah, thanks to your throttling that Riverside thug for me, but now Sandi is implying that I'm choosing wrestling over her."

"People choose things all the time. Most of the time, they aren't intentionally trying to anger people by doing so. It's like ..."

Patron stopped for a moment as if trying to figure out what to say. It seemed he needed to say something but was hesitant. Nick watched him carefully for several moments.

"Do you remember when we were freshmen and I got sent away?" Patron finally asked.

"Of course."

"Well, that was my mom's choice after I fought off her psycho boyfriend. I'll probably never talk to her again. She chose that scum bag over her own son. That's a pretty big deal. Choosing to wrestle even if it makes your girlfriend sad ... that's going to be forgotten two weeks from now."

Nick just nodded. In the grand scheme of things, his current issues suddenly seemed pretty minor.

"If you wrestle and lose, you'll still have a future. You'll still go to college. You'll still have those little kids cheering for you, and you'll still have an opening to be someone great. But if you let this beat you and give up, you'll be doing that for the rest of your life."

Nick looked at his fingers again. They were such a small part of his body and insignificant when he considered who he was and could be. He knew he would have to make a choice soon.

Chapter 66

Do you have time for lunch?"

Sean glanced up briefly from his computer screen but didn't make eye contact with the beautiful woman who had entered his workspace.

"That probably isn't such a good idea," he replied.

He had spent the morning in HR with his boss, his personnel file open and his employment agreement notably on top.

"According to our records," the HR Manager said snidely, "management had a long talk with you about keeping your nose clean when you started. Assaulting a co-worker's husband is what most of us would consider dripping with snot."

Other than firmly noting that he hadn't assaulted anyone and that, in the unlikely event that the case were to ever go to trial, he would be found innocent, Sean largely held his tongue. It was an uncomfortable meeting as the two men brought up Sean's tenuous employment status and that, if he were to stay employed, the smallest misstep would lead to his dismissal for cause in which case he would immediately have to pay back his loan.

Whether or not having lunch with Enid would be considered a misstep was debatable, but he was pretty sure that no good could come from it.

"I really need to talk to you about Friday," she pleaded.

He had never seen her in this kind of disarray. As his chivalrous instincts kicked in, he reluctantly agreed to meet her at a restaurant several blocks away where they were unlikely to be seen by co-workers.

* * *

Enid's story wasn't overly complex. She and Gary had been separated for over six months as he had struggled with mental health issues which drove him to rage at times.

"I appreciate that you didn't hurt him," she had told Sean. "He really can be sweet and doesn't need any more health problems."

Sean's mind went back to the hallway fight. He had assumed that Enid shouting, "Don't hurt him," was meant to protect himself, not the guy attacking him.

"I don't need any more problems either," Sean replied. "But suddenly I have a lawsuit hanging over my head which could land me in the unemployment line and lead me to financial ruin."

"He was only there that night to protect me from my creepy neighbor," Enid continued. "He assumed you were the creep from the fourth floor I had been telling him about in our recent phone conversations and got angry when he saw us walk in together."

Oddly, Sean had assumed that Gary was said creep.

"I'll talk to him about how you were only there to get me home safely, but it may take a few more days to get him to a place where he understands that you were only hitting him because you thought you needed to protect me."

"It will be nice to get some closure," he commented. "I'm walking on eggshells these days and am paranoid that, if I even get a speeding ticket on my trip this weekend, I may end up getting fired."

Any attempt Enid could make to get this cleaned up was welcomed by Sean. He just hoped that they could put this to rest quickly so that he could regain some stability. His mind crept back to two years earlier when he had ventured out in sub-zero temperatures in the middle of the night to give Mandi and her friends a ride home and was rewarded for his heroics by having a beer bottle broken over his head; resulting in a concussion. He hadn't really talked to the woman after that and their whole relationship was probably still reverberating through his life years later. Even incomplete closure with this Enid situation made him feel like he was in a better place.

Chapter 67

Troftgruben is a cheater," Ron's voice proclaimed over the phone. "He's scared of taking on real competition, so he flunked to wrestle younger, less physically and emotionally mature wrestlers. Now he's cutting weight because he thinks he can get in your head and intimidate you."

Nick suddenly wished he was heavier. He had heard of wrestlers who cut a lot of water weight adding back five to ten pounds between weigh-in and their first match. He wondered how much more Chester would weigh than himself if the two were to cross paths in the state tournament but then pondered that it didn't matter. Several of the 160-pounders he had wrestled over the season had likely done the same thing ... and Nick had still prevailed, winning the pre-Christmas tournament at 160.

"But you're going to beat him, Nick. You're going to beat him the way you beat everybody else," Ron continued.

"How is that?" Nick asked, getting agitated that his brother was suddenly the great guru of all things related to Nick.

"Don't be a dork," Ron huffed. "In your entire life, you've never been able to out-muscle anybody. Chimpanzees and other lower primates can out-think you ..."

"A pep talk, complete with insults," Nick thought.

"... but in your entire life, I've never met anyone who can out-work you. Tenacity is the best tool you've got in your toolbox and it's all you need to bury Troftgruben and everyone else whose path crosses yours at state. How many extra hours of workouts have you had this year?"

"You mean more than I usually ..."

"No," Ron interrupted. "I'm not comparing you to you. I mean how many more than the other guys on your team."

Nick thought about it.

"I'm estimating five hours a week, is that right?" Ron pushed.

"Well ..." Nick started.

"So let's say it's only four," Ron cut in again. "And there are 15 weeks in wrestling season so that means you put in an extra 60 hours this season, probably 200 extra in the off-season, and you've been doing that as much as your body will allow for years."

"But Chester ..."

"Chester shows up for camps, but back when he and I went to camp together after my freshman year, he was just going through the motions. He was there to be seen by potential recruiters, for a light workout and for the social aspects. The guy is going to end up working in a job where he can be all personality and appearance and not have to think or put in any extra effort."

"Enough about Chester," Nick finally said, not wanting to think of him. He silently hoped that the western wrestler would lose a fluke match in the tournament and enable Nick to avoid facing the state's other top candidate for "Mr. Wrestling."

"I should probably get going to pick up mom anyway," Ron changed the subject.

Their mom was on an east-bound plane to spend a few days over parents' weekend with her older son while their dad would leave the farm for the weekend to be in the stands for Nick at the state tournament. The two had joked that they were glad they had stopped after having two kids as trying to fit in travel for a third would be impossible.

There was a moment of awkward silence as the two pondered how to end the call.

"Wish me luck," Nick finally muttered.

"You don't need luck," his brother countered. "Just go out and win your matches one at a time. Bring home the gold."

"Ok, I'll see you soon," Nick added.

His fingers caught his attention as he hung up.

He may not need luck, but right now he was willing to take whatever he could get.

Chapter 68

Nick looked down the hallway. It was two days until the state tournament and he suddenly felt ill-prepared.

He had rested on Sunday as the doctor had ordered, but when he woke up Monday morning, his fingers continued bleeding each time he removed the pressure of the gauze and bandages. Monday's and Tuesday's practices had found him half working-out. He would ride the stationary bike or run laps – attempting to keep his conditioning up to par despite not being able to wrestle live.

By the time he woke up Wednesday morning, he was feeling lethargic, not even wanting to climb out of bed. His substandard workouts weren't keeping him at his usual level of fitness, while his diet had languished a few days as he sought comfort foods to help get past missing Sandi.

Sandi.

Nick couldn't get his mind off the girl. He felt like a loser for failing in the relationship and felt like a chump for missing the signs that something was wrong. He wondered if he would have taken to heart Oscar's warning had the message come from anyone other than Oscar. How could he ever possibly make a relationship work if he had botched things so badly with the perfect woman?

"Get moving," the voice had told him. It was the little voice that chided him every time he let himself get lazy. He liked to think it was Dino somehow reaching out to him, but perhaps it had been getting after him longer than that.

He complied.

Twenty minutes and a cold carride later, Nick stood in the hallway at South, staring down the corridor at those aged marble floors in the dim pre-dawn light.

"Do it," the voice commanded.

Nick leapt forward, starting at a manageable pace and slowly increasing his speed.

"I've never met anyone who can out-work you." Ron's words echoed in his mind.

By the time he got to the end of the first hall and bolted up the stairs, he knew that he would give it all in this workout and propel himself toward the state tournament.

The world could take his girl, take his health and take his confidence, but he was resolute on giving everything he had in a final push. The world could NOT take his dream ... at least not until the weekend.

* * *

"Hi, Mrs. Davis. May I speak to Sandi, please?"

Nick hoped he didn't sound too nervous. He was petrified as he sat in his basement and waited for the response.

"One minute, Nick ..." the woman replied.

He tried to read into her tone. She sounded like she was rushing. Was she irritated that he was calling Sandi now that the two of them had broken up? Was she still mad at him for not eating enough when he had come over for dinner?

Voices in the background distracted him. He strained to discern whose voices they were and make out what they were saying. One of the voices was male. Nick initially assumed that it was Sandi's dad, but then fear overwhelmed him as he realized it could be someone else. Could it be Aidan?

He fidgeted and forced himself to resist the urge to head for the bathroom. He and Sandi had talked briefly the prior night and she had used the "f" word ... "friends" ... the last word Nick wanted to hear. But he imagined that staying friends had to be better than not having her in his life at all going forward.

It seemed like the chatter lasted for hours, but eventually Sandi picked up the phone.

"Hi Nick. How are you?"

Her voice was sympathetic. It was the same tone a person would use when checking on someone after a close relative died.

"I'm good, how are you?"

"Really busy. I've got a ton of homework tonight."

"Me too," he lied. The boy had completed every last bit of homework while avoiding making this phone call. Yet, he now felt rushed. He needed to ask his question before she could find a reason to hang up.

"Um ... I know we're not ... not really going out any more. But I was ... I was hoping that you would come to watch me at state."

He took a deep breath and realized that her taking two days plus driving time was a lot to ask.

"... only the championship match," he continued. "It would really mean a lot if you were there."

Her silence was deafening as he paced, waiting for an answer. If only she would say "yes", he could go into the tournament with some kind of renewed self-confidence.

"I don't know that this is a good idea," she finally replied.

"I know it's a lot to ask and it's a four-hour drive, but I wrestle my best when you're there and I would win the match for you."

"Nick, don't ..."

"I know it's kind of weird and I know you don't like wrestling, but this is the biggest tournament of my life, and I love you and I want you to be a part of it."

"Nick, I can't."

"Just say you'll consider it," he pushed. He could feel the tears welling up and his hand was shaking so hard that he could barely hold onto the phone. "We don't have to go out afterward or anything but it would mean a lot if you could be there, just for the one match. My mom can't go so you could sit in her reserved seat."

"Nick, I'll say I'll consider it but I really can't do this. I need to go do homework. You need to do homework. You take care of you this weekend. Don't get hurt. I've got to go."

"Sandi ..."

The line went dead and he went to re-dial but held himself back.

"It's over. She's not coming," he told himself.

His heart got tight and he bit the knuckles of his trembling right hand.

All was lost. He needed to find some way to recover his shattered self esteem in the 36 hours before the state tournament started.

Chapter 69

The trio of wrestlers and their coach had largely ridden four hours in silence. The three boys' heads were filled with thoughts of winning the state title. They had each worked too hard to settle for anything less than a championship plaque.

Yet, each was truly a longshot. Seagull would face the top seed in the first round; Tanner would be seeded third at 145, and Nick would be second to Troftgruben at 152. Knowing that even with full use of his fingers, Nick had never beaten Chester, he was doing his best to not resign himself to a second-place finish. Then again, in his weakened condition, he acknowledged the risk that he could be upset in an early round.

"Shake it off," he thought. "You've come too far to let things end like that."

So, for the entire trip, the group kept mainly to themselves, lost in their thoughts, earphones on, each listening to his own music while Coach Nestor listened to NPR on the radio. Occasional conversations were short-lived.

It wasn't until after arriving in the capital city and checking weight that their coach pulled them all together for a serious discussion.

"This isn't public knowledge," the coach started, "but I think the three of you should know that this will be the final year of the South High School wrestling program. Our city has been shrinking over the past decade and the number of students and wrestlers at both South and Riverside has shrunk accordingly as families have moved away so parents can look for better job prospects."

Nick thought of the Riverside glory years as his coach spoke. Yes there were still kids coming up but he remembered stories of having so many wrestlers in the program that the high school fielded multiple teams. For his entire high school career, both schools had struggled to fill all of the weight classes.

"I've had several meetings with the administration of both high schools as well as the Riverside coaching staff. This fall, we will combine our programs into a single Riverside / South program in order to field a more competitive team and decrease our financial losses."

Nick's mind drifted back to his conversation with Sandi about seeing Nestor at Riverside and his own experience with the Riverside principal and coach touring the South wrestling room. Suddenly, it all made sense. He simultaneously felt remorse and pride. He mourned the loss of the programs that had meant so much to him since his youth while feeling the accomplishment of being a trend-setter who showed that a wrestler could be successful in both programs.

It didn't change his goal for the weekend but did add greater meaning to the title he sought.

Chapter 70

Nick stood beside the mat, awaiting his first match ever at a state tournament.

On a neighboring mat to his left, Oscar completed a Grandby roll and escaped for a point while simultaneously, to Nick's right, Chester plowed into an opponent, pushing and pulling the boy before setting him up and completing a throw.

Nick absorbed none of it. His warm-up hood was up, hiding his headphones which blared Ozzy Osbourne's *Crazy Train* in his ears.

In his little island of reality, there were no former friends competing in the same tournament. There were no fans, bloody fingers or possible excuses for losing.

Coach Nestor tapped him on the back and he mechanically shed his warm-ups and music, fluidly strapping on his headgear as he strode out to the center of the mat.

The match started with Nick shooting immediately and taking his opponent down. The well-conditioned "Mr. Wrestling" candidate controlled the entire match, broke only a minor sweat, and showed no emotion at the end of the bout when his hand was raised in victory.

He was on the final mile of his journey. There was no room for distractions.

Chapter 71

Tanner hopped around beside the mat, getting his blood flowing and steadying his focus on his upcoming opponent. He had made the quarter-finals and this, like all matches going forward, was a match he needed to win.

"Tanner Nestor, state champion," he thought. This was the weekend. This was the tournament that would give him a chance to follow in his father's footsteps. Winning this state title would give him a shot at tying his dad's record. Winning this year and either of the next two years would earn him as many state titles, or possibly even more than the Castle brothers combined. Nick winning a title this year wasn't guaranteed by any means. Could Tanner surpass his teammate in this tournament alone?

Waiting on deck, his mind raced. Even with a tender shoulder, this match was his to win. As the match before him ended, he donned his headgear and stepped on the mat, knowing that he would win, guaranteeing that he would place in the tournament ... but placing wasn't enough. He needed to go all the way in order to meet his own expectations.

* * *

Nick looked into the stands again. The smiling cheering faces that greeted him did nothing to lighten his mood. He looked away, searching ...

His second-round match had been more difficult than his first-round 9 – 3 victory in which he had only given up escapes. Plus, the second round had started to show some wear on his fingers. After his hand was raised, he had tried to be covert about glancing down at them. There was a mild stinging sensation and he could see the blood soaking through the bandages. He tried not to be too concerned despite his doctor's words echoing through his skull, "... those fingers will become a painful, mangled mess." It seemed to be the trajectory on which they were headed.

The fingers and his relatively-narrow 6 – 3 second round victory were not what caused him to be on edge. He was living his dream, progressing forward round-after-round in the state tournament ... and felt completely empty.

Sandi had not shown up. Of course, she said she wouldn't, but Nick continued to hold out hope. Patron apparently hadn't been able to weasel his way out of school and, if he had, it probably wouldn't have mattered as the boy didn't have transportation for the long drive.

A brief thought passed through his mind regarding Coach MacCallister and the mystery postcard from the prior spring. It had to have been from his coach, yet there had been no sign of that young man either. What bothered Nick the most was the absence of his own father. His dad had only missed a handful of matches throughout Nick's career. Why was it that, in the most important tournament of the boy's life, he looked up in the stands only to find that his parents' reserved seats were empty.

Coach Nestor patted Nick on the back as he left the mat before running off to Seagull's match. Nick was on his way, but he was traveling alone.

Chapter 72

Sean raced down the stairs with a travel mug full of coffee and a travel bag full of work papers that would ensure that he didn't have a free moment all weekend.

In his work environment, surprises were constant. Sean had asked for Thursday and Friday off two months in advance and they had been granted. Yet, the executives had chosen to schedule a review meeting to discuss both the completed and ongoing phases of project Roadrunner for Friday morning. This, of course, meant that Sean would not only be unable to leave Thursday to travel to the state wrestling tournament, he would miss all Friday sessions and have to drive all night. He could only hope and pray that Nick would wrestle well the first day so that Sean could see him wrestle Saturday.

The coffee would help ensure that the young man would stay awake for at least the first portion of the 14 hour trip. This made the Mustang the bigger concern. It had not been driven on a trip of this length since Sean had resurrected it from its dilapidated condition. With Sean's TLC and a few minor hour-long road tests it seemed like it would perform, but time and distance would tell the story.

Having not slept much the prior week while preparing for Friday's meeting, Sean knew he would have to sleep somewhere along the way or, at minimum, once he reached his destination.

He jumped into the car, turned the key in the ignition, and listened to the Mustang engage to a powerful growl.

"This is it, girl. People are counting on us. It's all up to you now."

He put the car in gear, turned on some Jim Croce, took a sip of coffee and began rolling toward his destination.

Chapter 73

He sat sulking after his semi-final loss, beating on himself for being stupid and lamenting the lost opportunity to bring home a state championship.

After racking up a 10 – 3 lead, he had seen an opening, gotten too aggressive, lost his balance and instead of putting his opponent's shoulders to the mat, he had pinned himself.

"Stupid, stupid, stupid," he thought. It was his chance to get to the state title match and he had squandered it. Worse yet, in doing so, he had tweaked his neck and shoulder. Something wasn't right in there but he would grit it out through what would now be two more matches.

"Tanner," his dad's voice called and the boy cringed.

"I've got to get to Nick's match," his dad continued, "but wanted you to know that, while you nearly gave me a heart attack at the end, you wrestled a heck of a match."

Tanner just nodded as his dad stroked the boy's hair once and walked away.

It was all made worse by the fact that Oscar had been Tanner's opponent. That arrogant creep was going to the state championship and all Tanner could do was wait for next year.

Chapter 74

Not gonna happen, Rodham!" Nick thought as he blocked his opponent's attempt to turn him. It was the state semi-finals and Castle led 7 – 5 over Danny Rodham, the sixth seed, in the third period.

The boy tried to keep his mind off of his fingers while at the same time protecting them. In the quarter-finals, Nick's opponent had grabbed Nick's fingers while Castle was stuck on the bottom and sent a shearing pain through his right hand, causing him to give up a point when he shoved the boy in retaliation.

"It's wrestling," the ref had told Nick. "It was your choice to wrestle while injured ... deal with it."

From that point on, Nick had gone on the offensive, using his superior conditioning to rack up four unanswered points and win 7 – 3. He carried that momentum into his semi-final but, as the third period waned, he became more defensive.

"Warning, stalling," the ref called, tapping on the mat.

Unwilling to give up a point unnecessarily while milking a two-point lead, Castle donned a determined look and worked back up to his base.

For the rest of the match, he was able to counter his opponent's attack and move upward.

"Not gonna happen, Rodham!" he thought time after time including during one last rally as time expired.

It was neither his most impressive match nor one that showed his true potential. Yet, what was important was that he had won the match which was a gateway to the state championship.

Chapter 75

Sean smiled as he stared across the table at Nick. The young man was sobering up nicely and progressing to an almost jovial mood.

It had been over two hours since the two had run into each other and, for the first time in several weeks, Sean remembered what it felt like to feel good about something he had accomplished in life. This imperfect college senior in front of him had gone from being an ultra-shy underachiever the first half of his high school sophomore year to one of the premier wrestlers in the state as a junior and beyond. In some small way, surely Sean had played a role in that.

Based on Nick's tales from college, he had continued to grow and mature in his adult years, not letting life's inevitable setbacks get the better of him. He had red-shirted on the university wrestling team as a freshman and continued wrestling there through his junior year but had not regularly appeared on the starting roster. Sean saw some of himself in Nick. You get knocked down, you get back up. You get knocked down again, you get back up again. Repeat, and repeat, and repeat ... at least until the load gets to be too much.

He shook his head, not allowing the dark thoughts to get the better of him. He quickly distracted himself by thinking back to the last time he had seen Nick.

"What do you remember most about that match?" Sean asked, taking a sip of his tea.

He wasn't ready for the response.

"I remember that I wanted to die," Nick replied.

Sean almost choked on the tea as he saw Nick's eyes grow distant and fog over a bit. He waited for what seemed like minutes before continuing, looking past Sean as he spoke.

"I remember that I was up by one point in the third ... and he got the reversal. I remember fighting with everything I had to get away and begging God and myself to just help me find the escape. I remember that fog horn blowing and I was still on the bottom and it was like my soul was torn out of me. And I remember lying

there, face down in front of all of those people and wishing I could disappear but, more importantly, wishing I could just die."
    Sean had no idea how to respond.

Chapter 76

William Castle's heart ached as he hung up the phone, leaving his younger son to suffer alone, hundreds of miles away.

The elder Castle shook his head, haunted by Nick's final words to him and the fear and desperation in the boy's voice.

The man could only think of three more gut-wrenching events in his life – the night of Ron's accident three years earlier, the afternoon the previous summer when he was informed about his father unexpectedly passing away, and the early-morning news about Dino's murder.

How this day could be as solemn as those three had never crossed William's mind when he had awoken that morning. His biggest fear at that point was that Nick's fingers would cause the boy to exit the state tournament prematurely, ending his illustrious high school career without placing at state.

With all of the success that Nick had earned, so many still considered the boy the constant underdog, the little guy who had to go out and slay giants. Yet, so many athletes and teams had found ways to defy the odds. He thought of the Green Bay Packers – the smallest franchise in the NFL had more world championships than any other team. Similarly, the University of North Dakota had a student body a fraction of the size of most of the teams it faced in Division One Hockey, yet the Fighting Sioux had hung more national championship banners since 1959 than any other team. Could Nick fare the same way?

This had been the only real concern on his mind starting the previous afternoon when William had given the boy a big bear hug before the two parted ways – Nick to head toward the capital city for the state tournament and William to head the opposite direction to pick up some replacement parts for his aged cultivator prior to spring planting.

William had gotten a great deal on the parts, purchasing them from his retiring uncle 100 miles to the east who had talked William into spending the night.

Leaving his uncle's farm early in the morning, William knew that he had plenty of time to make it home, drop off the parts, and get on the road to watch Nick wrestle. But, upon arriving home, he was immediately concerned when Chewie didn't run out to greet him.

He spent over an hour searching the farmstead and then drove slowly down the gravel road, calling the dog's name and hoping that he would come running out at any time.

By mid-afternoon, William knew that he would be missing some of Nick's matches but also knew that the boy would be devastated if he showed up at the tournament and had to announce that the dog was missing. Thus, he continued his search, on foot, walking through the snow-filled ditches until he finally saw pale gold fur amidst the dirty white snow.

He initially assumed that the animal was dead but, as he approached, Chewie opened an eye, lightly wagged his tail for a moment, and whimpered in pain. The vet arrived an hour later, securing the dog for a trip to the clinic where he would confirm that Chewie had been hit by some kind of vehicle, breaking the dog's hip and crushing his left rear leg.

Whether or not the right thing to do was to put the dog to sleep, William didn't know. What he did know was that it would be cruel to let him live and possibly just as cruel to end Chewie's life without giving Nick a chance to say "goodbye."

As much as he hated to do so, William called Nick late that night to let him know that the dog was going into surgery but likely wouldn't make it based on the extensive internal damage. He suggested that he could drive to the capital city that night, but could hear the pain and tears in his son's voice as the boy pleaded.

"Don't, Dad. Don't let him die alone. Just don't let him die alone."

His heart in ruins, Nick's father returned to the veterinary clinic and kept watch over his son's dog. He would not abandon his family members, not even the dirty, furry one.

Chapter 77

Nick sat at mat-side, watching Tanner wrestle for third. Something wasn't right with his teammate; the boy was wrestling tentative and Nick was the only one who knew the reason why.

Earlier that afternoon, Nick had caught Tanner taking pills after his previous match, which the boy had wrestled in similar fashion but still had come out on top.

"I just have this numbness, that's all," the boy had told him in confidence when Nick pressed him. "I just need to stretch my neck and shoulder and tough it out for one more match. It will be fine. DON'T tell my dad."

Despite his initial concern, the look in Tanner's eyes told Nick that he was prepared to wrestle through the pain, just like Nick would be doing in another two and a half hours with crushed fingers in the finals. He told himself that, if they wrestled smart, there would be nothing to worry about. But his concern escalated as he noted how slowly Tanner was responding to his opponent's attack. He was grinding it out but not doing an acceptable job of protecting himself.

With the match still scoreless going into the third, Tanner's opponent had chosen the bottom position. The bright side of this was that the boy couldn't twist Nestor around quite as easily as he had in the second period. The coach's kid looked clumsy as he tried to ride. He was hanging on for dear life and nearly lost his grip before the two grapplers ended up off the mat.

Tanner was slow to get up but returned to the center of the mat. His dad signaled him to ride legs, and the boy stiffly nodded in response.

As the bottom man tried to escape, Tanner awkwardly put in both legs and tried to ride. His opponent, feeling that Tanner was getting too high and losing control, got to his feet and hands like a bear and, before the ref could signal "potentially dangerous," dived and rolled forward.

It took place in the flash of an eye but was a moment that would be burned into Nick's brain for the remainder of his life. Tanner came down head first into the mat. His neck snapped back as his body continued its path, slamming to the mat and lying still as the crowd let out a collective gasp.

"Tanner!" Coach Nestor yelled as he sprinted to the mat to his motionless son. A swarm of trainers and medical staff joined him as they tried to do something, anything to revive the motionless wrestler.

Paramedics were on the scene within minutes and braced the boy's neck before putting him on a gurney. He didn't open his eyes. His father joined him in the ambulance, which sped away with a whole stadium of fans watching in silence.

All Nick could do was pray that his teammate would be all right as the guilt of not ratting out the boy began gnawing at his insides.

Chapter 78

Sean wandered into a new section, trying to figure out the best way to get down to mat-side. It was his third pass around the facility and he had looked down on the arena floor from every angle. Surely Nick would be down there somewhere. The brackets showed him as making it into the championship match but MacCallister was losing hope. He just couldn't get close enough to find the boy.

The place seemed like a war zone. Security guards in each section kept an eye on the crowd and ensured that nobody without a pass made it to the arena floor. A year earlier, a spectator had gotten into a fight with and injured a wrestler, thus creating an uproar and call for tighter protection.

His plight looked daunting. MacCallister continued his search, getting more aggravated by the minute. He had driven over 800 miles in a car that failed just about every road-safety measure and now wasn't even going to get to see Nick? Sean had noted only one place that held potential, a dark secluded corner where he could hang from a railing and drop … but it was a long way down. He would keep it in mind as a last resort.

As he squeezed past some on-coming fans and a yellow-shirted security guard, he made a point of looking nobody in the eye. There was no way he was going to return home without making sure that Nick knew he had come to watch … the trick would be in doing so without getting arrested.

"MacCallister. Are you looking for the kid?"

Sean whirled at the sound of his name. He immediately recognized the gravely voice but, searching the crowd, he could not find Coach Granger's face.

"Down here," the man continued.

Sean looked over the railing to find Granger, dressed in a security guard's outfit but otherwise looking as worn and disheveled as he had two years earlier when the two had coached together.

MacCallister smiled at the sight of the old man but smiling wasn't in Granger's DNA.

"Security guard?" Sean asked.

"It's a job," came the reply.

"Do you know how I can find Nick?"

"He's bound to be somewhere down there on the floor. His teammate, Nestor's kid, went down in the third-place match. Nasty injury ... looked serious ... the ambulance drove him away and Nestor went with him. I doubt he'll be back. Castle is probably moping around there somewhere trying to get his head on straight for the finals ... never was much good at that."

Leave it to Granger to find something negative to say.

"Can you get me down there to see him?"

"I can, but I'd lose my job if anyone sees me."

The old man looked around.

"It's amazing to me that the kid made it this far. Every time I see him step out on the mat, I cringe and wonder how he's going to find a way to lose. The kid he's wrestling is a meat head but at least he looks like a true grappler. Every match in this tournament, Castle had to grind it out. He looks like he's on death's door. But at the same time, I heard that a bunch of coaches are waiting until after the 152-pound final to submit their votes for Mr. Wrestling. The kid must be doing something right."

"I just need to talk to him for a minute so that he knows I'm here to watch him."

Granger pondered for a moment.

"You know, my shift is done in ten minutes. Meet me by the stairs in five. I get paid whether anyone gets by me or not so we may as well get you down there to talk to the kid one last time..."

Sean momentarily pondered whether the former Riverside coach was getting soft in his old age before the old man derailed Sean's thoughts.

"... by the time the finals are over, you'll probably need dental records to identify him."

Chapter 79

Nick sat on the warm-up mat. It was nearly two hours until the finals under the big lights at the capital city's civic center but the boy was already dressed in his warm-ups with his slick black championship singlet underneath.

He wished that something had gone right ... anything had gone right.

The queasy feeling in his stomach continued to get worse as he worried about Tanner. Would the boy be ok? Nick dreaded the thought of wrestling in the championship without Coach Nestor ... or any coach for that matter but knew that his coach's place had to be at the hospital with his son.

Not embarrassing himself while wrestling Chester would be a difficult proposition for Nick under ideal circumstances, but doing it without a coach and with smashed fingers that were semi-worthless made the ordeal look completely hopeless.

Then, there was the talk of the "Western Sweep." Nick was one of only three eastern conference wrestlers to make the finals. In a tournament hosted in the heart of the western half of the state, fans were eager to see their wrestlers take home every title. With Oscar already winning by default, the fans would be cheering for the blood of the two remaining eastern wrestlers so that they could at least claim that the west had won every championship match.

The thought of Oscar being a state champion nauseated Nick. The boy with the bad attitude whom Nick had never seen work for anything in his life was going to be joining Riverside's Ring of Honor due to his would-be opponent blowing out his knee as time expired in his semi-final match. Yet, for all of the success Nick had spent countless hours earning, he was unlikely to hoist the gold plaque by the end of his career.

Why hadn't Nick just bit his lip and wrestled at state his junior year? Was the sacrifice for a coach he hadn't seen in the past year worth it? For the first time, he seriously questioned his own judgment on the matter, feeling completely alone and foolish, just as the voice rang in his ears.

"Nick?"

The boy froze and shook his head, wondering why the sudden thoughts of his former coach had made him conjure up the young man's voice in his head.

"Nick?" Sean's voice repeated.

The boy turned around, not knowing what to say as he came face-to-face with his hero and mentor.

* * *

Sean was elated to finally get to see the boy. Nick had sprouted up over the past year and was probably another inch taller. With so much to talk about, he didn't know where to start.

"What happened to your fingers?" Sean asked, looking at the digits wrapped heavily in tape.

Nick just shook his head, "Got in an unfortunate fight with a van door."

MacCallister was a bit nervous to be in such a precarious situation. Granger had trudged off and Sean was pretty sure there would be some kind of trespassing charge if he were to get caught on the arena floor. He didn't know what kind of trouble he could get into for that but was pretty sure it would be less severe than the penalty for violating the year-old restraining order by talking to Nick. Kreitzer had gotten the restraining order the prior February when Sean had been fired from Riverside and this was the first time since that he had been around any of his former wrestlers.

Sean searched for an escape route. Perhaps he and Nick could line up some time after the match to get together and talk. He had delivered on his promise to be at the state tournament, but he also needed to find ways to stay out of jail.

"Can you coach me?"

Sean's jaw dropped. How poorly timed was this question?

"I'm a bit out of practice ..." he began to explain before Nick cut him off.

"You don't really need to coach me, but if you could be in my corner, that would be great. It's all kind of overwhelming, and I don't know that I can go out there all alone."

Sean knew what it felt like to be the little guy, all alone, defending his team from corporate executives and whatever external forces were able to have their say regarding his project. He remembered going into a meeting and just wishing his VP would be there as one person who wasn't against him, but of course the VP didn't show up. Nick's pressure had to be a hundred times what Sean had felt given the entire civic center was filled with fans that would likely favor Nick's western conference opponent. Could Sean truly retreat to the safety of the stands and watch the boy struggle alone?

"I'll be there for you, Nick. I won't let you down."

The boy let out a nervous grin, looking like someone sentenced to death who was just given a reprieve. Yet, he didn't exude the confidence of someone about to step onto the mat for the biggest match of his life.

"Do you have all of the tools you'll need to win?" Sean pressed. "You need to start focusing now, if you haven't been already, on what you're bringing to the match and why you're going to beat this kid."

He could see Nick's wheels begin to turn at the same time he himself realized that he hadn't brought a change of clothes or even a razor and that he'd look fairly shabby out there at mat-side, probably sticking out like a sore thumb for people like Kreitzer to notice and call the authorities.

The two talked for a couple more minutes and it suddenly felt like old times again.

"What do you remember most about the years you coached us?" Nick asked.

Sean pondered the question for a moment before a voice rang out in his ears.

"HEY YOU!!!"

Sean turned to see a heavy-set security guard ambling his way.

"Where are your credentials?" the guard asked.

"I must have left them in the coaches' room when we were playing cards," Sean lied, casting an uneasy glance at Nick.

"Well, let's just see about that, Buddy," the guard stated, taking Sean by the elbow and marching him toward a hallway. "They'd better be there or you're in big trouble, mister ..."

Looking for a way out, Sean eyed some escalators and, breaking from the security guard's grip, he sprinted for and bounded up the 'down' escalator, making his escape while the pudgy man yelled out behind him.

With all of the other tournament noise, the guards at the top of the escalator didn't hear their colleague's calls and barely noticed Sean as he strode into the civic center lobby and wondered how he would possibly get back down to the arena floor to coach Nick.

Chapter 80

Sean walked through the halls of the Capital City civic center, weaving through the crowd and considering his next move. He wished he had packed a suit. He wished that he had time and a razor to shave. In short, he wished there was some way, any way, for him to disguise himself so as to blend in.

At least he had half a plan, which was certainly better than no plan at all. He would wait another ten minutes until the 130-pound match to make his descent. The arena corners were fairly dark giving him some good options for sneaking down undetected. He would need to slip through the railing, hang momentarily by his arms and drop to the floor below. It would still be a five to six-foot drop but there was minimal possibility of injury. He had used the same hang and drop technique hundreds of times as a kid while playing in trees in his grandparents' yard.

After that, he would find his way back to Nick, prep the boy for the match and hopefully not run into the same security guard who had grabbed him earlier. There would still be some degree of risk as he did not have the official credentials hanging on a lanyard around his neck, but hopefully nobody would notice that.

"What about other coaches?" he pondered. He had gotten to know a number of the other high school coaches over his two seasons at Riverside. There was always the chance that one of them would point out that he didn't belong in the secure area. It was a minor risk but certainly one to keep in mind.

Thoughts of avoiding anyone he might know were still reverberating in his mind when he heard it.

"Mac? Mac, is that you?"

Surprisingly, it wasn't his being recognized that scared him nearly as much as the excited, happy voice calling out to him. He turned his head twenty degrees and came face-to-face with Mandi Isaacson.

"Mac, it is you. I haven't seen you in years."

At a time when he didn't want to be seen, why did his name need to be yelled down the hall? She was coming straight toward him and he was left with the awful choice of turning and running, certain to draw plenty of looks, or suffering through a conversation with the woman he least wanted to see.

"Uh, hey Mandi," he started. What on earth could he say to her that was the least bit authentic yet still polite? His mind drifted back two years to the night he had ventured out to retrieve her from a night club, only to end up getting his skull busted open with a beer bottle. Clearly, the woman hadn't intended to draw him into a dangerous situation; but, intended or not, Sean had ended up in the hospital with scars he would wear for the rest of his life.

"I can't believe it's you," she continued. "Do you live here now? Did you finish school? I didn't. I quit after junior year ... had to get my life back in order ... too much partying ... needed to study more, needed stability."

Sean could hardly keep up with the string of dialogue but couldn't disagree with any of the statements. He sincerely hoped that this new environment had helped her the same way his move from the party-heavy university town had helped him.

"No, I moved out of state, I'm just back for state wrestling. One of my former wrestlers is in the state finals."

He looked around sheepishly, trying to find a way out but only found the face of the one person he feared running into even more than Mandi — Kreitzer.

Sean tried to become invisible as the man walked his direction, talking with someone who was undoubtedly a tournament official or key player among the state's board of higher education. Kreitzer had his usual "suck up" look on his face, undoubtedly trying to use this opportunity to gain political clout. If they saw him, Sean was sure to be called out and Nick would be abandoned, left without a coach.

How had Sean not thought of this? Why hadn't he looked into the details of the restraining order? If it were effective for a year, with the state tournament moving forward a week, it would still be in effect or only expired by a day or two. Could he end up in jail tonight for coaching a wrestling match?

The look of panic displayed on the young man's face was clearly visible to Mandi.

"What's wrong?" she asked.

The only thing that outweighed his lack of trust in her was his need to remain unnoticed. He angled his body so that his back was to Kreitzer.

"The guy coming down the hall in the expensive-looking suit has it in for me. I just need to make sure he doesn't see me. Do you see him?"

"Yeah, I see him."

Mandi began moving to Sean's right as Kreitzer passed behind Sean, moving to his left.

"Does he see me?"

"No," Mandi replied, to Sean's relief. Then, to his concern, she continued, "He's totally checking me out."

It wasn't until after she had said the words that Sean noted how hot Mandi was looking. Clearly, any red blooded man would have been distracted by the beautiful woman and paid little to no attention to the man she was talking to.

Her eyes remained focused behind Sean for another several moments before returning to look him in the eye.

"Is he gone?"

"More or less. He is continuing down the hall but he's looked back twice already. What's his story?"

"It's a long and painful story, which probably ends up with me going to jail, losing my job and ending up destitute if he sees me coaching the 152-pound final."

"Is it a crime to coach?"

"No, but there are extenuating circumstances and, unfortunately, this kid doesn't have any other options for a coach."

"So are you saying that coaching this kid is worth risking everything? Would he do that for you? Normal people wouldn't do that."

The look on Mandi's face showed that she was seriously questioning his judgment. Yet at the same time, it did force Sean to reflect on how ludicrous the situation must seem to an outsider.

Even without concrete proof; Sean felt that, beyond a shadow of a doubt, if the roles were reversed, Nick would do the same for him.

"Maybe not normal people, but some people would ..."

Mandi cut him off before he could say any more.

"He's coming back. You better go."

Without another word, Sean continued down the hall, away from Kreitzer and toward his destiny.

Chapter 81

Sean looked nervously into the stands and tried to stay out of the bright lights. He had gotten to the arena floor undetected, finding a dark corner, hanging from the railings and dropping down where nobody would see him. Yet now, he was very close to taking center stage under the big lights. Would Kreitzer notice him and call him out? What about the security guard? Certainly one of them would create trouble for him at mat-side.

Hopefully, any trouble could wait until after Nick's match ... and Sean could find a way to escape one last time.

* * *

As the 140-pounders took the mat, the butterflies took wing in Nick's stomach. He ditched his warm-up bottoms as he continued to stretch. He looked in the stands one last time, hoping to find his dad or Sandi but the reserved seats were still empty.

"Chewie must have passed away," the boy thought sorrowfully.

He looked over at his coach. If anyone would know how to get rid of this nagging fear, it would be Coach MacCallister. Nick wondered what it was that was different about the man tonight as Sean looked around, almost as if he were on the run, expecting someone to come after him.

"I've lost my girl, and my dog," Nick thought. "Wrestling is the only thing left that still matters. I can't lose that, too."

Yet the horror in the back of his mind that he was about to be destroyed under the big lights wouldn't go away. He jumped up and made his way to his waiting coach, not knowing exactly what to say.

As he approached MacCallister, the man's focus changed, and suddenly his attention was completely on Nick.

"You feeling confident?" the man asked.

"Yeah," Nick lied.

Sean looked him in the eye.

"Come here," he said and Nick complied, joining the young man on the warmup mat.

Sean grabbed Nick's left arm and began shaking it out, never taking his gaze out of Nick's eyes.

"This is it," he coached. "Starting right now, everything else disappears. The only things that matter in this world are you, your opponent and the match. Shut everything else out."

He finished shaking out the left arm and grabbed Nick's right arm, careful to not jostle the boy's fingers.

"Nothing in the world is going to matter for the six minutes you are wrestling in that match ... nothing that has happened in any match this season, last season, or that crazy sophomore season of yours."

Nick smiled, glad to be getting his mind off of Chewie, Sandi, his fingers and his fears.

He had spent the past hour building up his own confidence and had come up with some reasons to believe he could win. Despite the nagging in the back of Nick's mind that told him that Chester couldn't be beaten, Chester had not only lost this year but he had lost to a wrestler that Nick had soundly beaten a year earlier. That had to point to Nick's favor.

Second, Chester's lone loss had come after cutting to 152, just like he had done again for the state tournament. When the boy had lost at the Capital tournament, he had essentially quit and not come back for the second day. Ron's words, "I've never seen anyone who can out-work you," came to mind. Nick knew he would need to keep Troftgruben from getting in his head and out-work the boy early in the match. If doing so would cause his opponent to get frustrated and "give up," Castle might have a shot.

Finally, Nick had not lost a match on the soil of his home state and thought of Ron's comment about Chester being scared. Nick was feeling strong at 152 and had been eating well while still easily making weight, which gave the dehydrated Troftgruben extra reason to think twice before believing Castle would fold easily. When he had wrestled Chester at camp the previous summer, he was giving up 15 pounds to the boy. That would not be the case tonight.

Nick didn't watch Oscar saunter out to center-mat to accept the forfeit and have his hand raised in victory. His petty squabbles with his former teammate didn't matter.

"Nothing else matters today," MacCallister continued. "This is your match. Go out and win it."

The boy's energy changed as he shut out the rest of the world and just let himself feel strong and unstoppable. Staying with his coach, he was able to keep the same focus as the seconds ticked down to his match ... and his destiny. Then all too soon, it was time for Nick to take the final step in pursuit of his dream.

Chapter 82

The two wrestlers faced each other; neither blinked. The packed civic center focused on two boys, both of whom seemed unbeatable – but only one would prove himself to be so tonight.

Jerry Broadsetter fidgeted in his general admission seat, trying not to appear too uncomfortable. It had been over a decade since the man had wrestled or been to a wrestling match. His last match was the state championship his senior year. It had broken his heart when he, for the second consecutive year, had ended his season as the "runner up." Twelve years of preparation had gone for naught that night. Jerry had never looked back.

Jerry felt the familiar tug on his left hand.

"Dad, is this the one?"

The man could barely hear his son's voice over the bustling of the crowd. It was for this reason and this reason alone that Jerry had been coaxed to watch the matches tonight. The six-year-old had gone to a high school dual with his uncles a month earlier, and they had filled him with stories about how unstoppable his old man had been. Daunte had decided that night that he would be a wrestler, too. Jerry had not had a moment of peace since.

"Yes, this is the one," Jerry finally replied. There had been so much buzz about the 152-pound title match: two wrestlers who were undefeated all season against in-state competition, two wrestlers who had placed at major national tournaments, two wrestlers who had become nearly mythical in the eyes of many in their hometowns, one of whom was going to go home devastated tonight.

He looked down at the competitors. The brawny, golden-haired Troftgruben looked like he should be a poster-child for the sport. Across from him, the gangly, awkward Castle looked downright ill in comparison. Jerry had seen Castle interviewed on TV after the Capital tournament the prior month and remembered thinking that the kid had the personality of a potato and should probably just quit now and find a job where he didn't have to be seen or heard.

"Who are we cheering for?" his son asked.

Jerry opened his mouth to answer "Troftgruben" before his son cut him off.

"I want the skinny, messy little boy to win," Daunte continued.

Jerry decided that he wouldn't ask why as it quickly sank in that, even in his own family, someone was going to go home disappointed tonight.

The whistle blew and the two wrestlers stepped forward. Troftgruben immediately tried to tie up with Castle which caused Nick to step backward, taking a defensive stance. As Chester advanced, Nick again took a step back. Then, out of nowhere, the South high school wrestler took a shot, drove his opponent off balance and spun around behind and on top of his opponent, right on the edge of the mat. The crowd's roar was deafening.

"No points," the ref yelled, signaling for "out of bounds."

"Let them wrestle on the edges!" Jerry didn't know if his boisterous remark surprised himself or his son more. He didn't want Castle to have the points but, at the same time, it looked to Jerry like a good takedown.

He put his arm around Daunte as he watched Castle's scruffy coach approach the referee to try to plead his wrestler's case, only to have his pleas fall on deaf ears.

The remainder of the first period treated the crowd to all they had hoped for. The two high school participants wrestling like college grapplers, both showing their ability to be aggressive while also showing a remarkable talent for countering the other's takedown attempts, even in the face of what appeared to be sure takedowns.

Jerry's attention was torn between watching the match and watching the mesmerized Daunte as the first period came to a close with the score still tied at 0 – 0.

Chapter 83

The ref flipped the coin which came up green, giving Chester the choice. He immediately deferred.

Without a word, Nick pointed down and moved to center mat, assuming bottom position on his hands and knees.

He closed his eyes and focused inward. There could be no distractions, no press, no crowd, just two high schoolers preparing for the final battle – one that may not only decide the state championship but also the state's "Mr. Wrestling."

Despite not scoring, Nick had gained some confidence in the first period. He had never before been able to keep up with Chester as he had during those two minutes. There had been several times when he had even been within a moment of scoring points on his friend. His endless hours poring over his combinations notebook had paid off. He needed to take his confidence and parlay it into some second-period points.

"Ready ... wrestle."

Nick was immediately moving forward with Troftgruben trying to break him down. After half a minute, he got his hips off to the side and tried coming out the back door but was cut off. Moving forward again, he sat out, was cut off again as Chester attempted a chin drop, and scrambled to the safety of his belly with Chester immediately on his back.

"Think, Castle, think ..." went through the boy's mind. "Not one move, think through combinations."

Sitting out a second time, Chester countered the same way but, instead of fleeing to his belly this time, Nick shifted his body, turning to face toward his opponent. Troftgruben immediately applied a head lock to Nick's head and right arm but at least Castle's legs and torso were free of the boy's weight.

Chester tried to spin around to Nick's left but was blocked by Castle's left arm.

"He's going to try to shuck me," Nick thought as he felt Troftgruben dragging him to the right, to the right, to the right ... gaining momentum until the shuck ...

It would have been more properly referred to as an attempted shuck as, at the exact moment when Chester tried to shuck him, Nick anticipated it, holding his position and letting his opponent go too far, losing control. When he did so, Castle took advantage of the opening, stopped the momentum Chester had built up, and got away.

"One point green," the ref declared as Nick found his way to his feet.

Chester was immediately on the attack again with Nick countering and trying to figure out how he would make it through the remaining fifty seconds of the period. Yet, there he was with a lead, somehow finding a way to stand toe-to-toe with his friend and opponent. Chester tried to muscle him, but Nick instinctively changed his stance and rebutted with offense attempting a duck-under and making Chester show some defensive reflexes of his own.

Even with a slight chill resonating through the civic center, the two boys began sweating from the relentless activity as both pursued this final match as if life itself were to only be preserved for the winner.

The second period ended with Nick leading 1 – 0.

Chapter 84

From Nick's corner, Sean's tension grew as he watched the match. He was amazed at how far the boy had come in the past year and wasn't sure what coaching advice he could possibly convey to someone with Nick's abilities.

For your average non-wrestling fan, the low-scoring match may have been looked upon as "boring," but Sean could feel the muscles on the back of his scalp straining as tension and excitement filled him. These two wrestlers were clearly in a class of their own and, judging by the focus of the sell-out crowd, everybody knew it.

The low scoring had not been driven by lack of aggression; it was just that the competitors were both so adept at countering that the constant action was not yielding points.

Chester pointed down for starting the final period and got set in the bottom position at center mat.

Sean recognized him from Nick's video from the prior year's pre-Christmas tournament. Yet, the chiseled wrestler's dominance on tape had not carried over into this contest. As sickly as Nick looked in comparaison, as the referee invited him to mount, he seemed to be every bit the competitor as his opponent having progressed much more impressively.

But would it be enough?

The whistle blew to begin the final two minutes and Nick, protecting his right fingers, immediately moved to break his opponent down. Chester tried for a switch but Nick followed through, coming back around behind him and remaining on top.

The coach was getting exhausted just watching the boys. He knew how hard Nick trained but was amazed at the boy's focus and stamina. Chester tried to flip Nick, but as Castle went over the top, he twisted and his feet instinctively found their way to the mat – immediately moving to the side, and within a second enabled him to scurry around behind again and remain in control. Clearly, the boy's flexibility and balance had improved over the past year as well.

As the match entered its final minute, Sean actually began to believe that Nick could actually beat this kid who had thrashed him so soundly the prior season.

Chapter 85

Nick contorted his body and somehow found a way to stay on top. He was dripping with sweat and stole an opportunity to wipe his left hand on Chester's singlet so that his hand didn't slip as badly. He was just under a minute from realizing his dream as he clung to the narrowest lead. Remaining focused, he countered another Troftgruben escape attempt, knowing that any scoring by the boy would result in a tie or worse.

"Watch your hands and keep them apart," he thought. The last thing he needed was to get called for clasping and give his opponent a point.

Seconds seemed like hours as they slowly ticked away. Nick put in a leg to give himself another grip and leverage point apart from his sweat-soaked arms.

Suddenly, Chester heaved his hips off to the side causing Nick to momentarily lose his balance.

A moment was all it took. As Nick scrambled to maintain control, Troftgruben came out the back door and toppled him, coming from behind and gaining control with 45 seconds remaining.

"Two points red!" the ref exclaimed as the crowd erupted.

Nick began to panic as he tried to sit through but felt Troftgruben block his progress.

"No!" he thought. "This can't be happening!"

A spasm of ice and adrenaline shot down Nick's spine. He panicked realizing that he trailed by a point, 1 – 2, with only forty clicks remaining. He tried to peel away from his opponent's grip but felt the boy's full weight on his back, draining his energy. For several more seconds he battled and felt fortunate to pull Chester out of bounds, forcing a fresh start.

Just 32 seconds remained as he scurried back to the center of the mat and got into referee's position.

The world disappeared until he heard the word "wrestle," at which point he again exploded.

"Up, up, up!" was the only thing on his mind. "Get away and force overtime!"

In all of his years, Nick had never strived so hard at the end of a match. He had no energy reserves left but still found a way to work upward as Chester asserted his superior weight and strength and did everything possible to hold him down. As Nick found his way to his feet and tried to gain hand control, he had a sensation that something had snapped in his right ring finger but continued pushing until Troftgruben angled him off the mat.

As Nick again moved to return to the center, he looked into his opponent's eyes. There was a look of agitated desperation on Chester's face and his eyes were almost teary.

"Stay down, Castle," the boy said and nodded toward Nick's fingers. Nick refused to look at his right hand and instead curled it into a fist. The match was waning. If his hand was going to end up dis-figured, nothing that could happen from here on out would make it much worse.

Coach MacCallister signaled to him to get up and shift his hips. Nick nodded in acknowledgement, knowing that the action was easier motioned than accomplished.

"Please God, just give me the strength for one last rally," he pleaded. "Just let me get away!"

Seven seconds remained. If he didn't escape, that seven seconds would be the final seven of his high school wrestling career, his dream and life as he knew it.

He got down in the bottom position, telling himself that he would give everything he had.

He felt Chester mount. The boy's body was to Nick's right side which would make things slightly more difficult due to Nick's splintered fingers. Troftgruben wiped a bit of sweat away near Nick's right elbow as he completed mounting.

"Up and out," Nick thought. "One last attempt."

Everything seemed to go in slow motion as Nick heard the referee's whistle.

"Up!" He told himself, his body already in motion, looking for a way out and getting straight to his feet with Chester hanging on for dear life.

"You can't hold on forever!" Nick's mind raced. If he had to carry the other boy with him, so be it, he thought as he powered his way to his feet, only to be thrown back to the mat again by the stronger boy.

The fog horn sounded in unison with the loudest crowd noise Nick Castle had ever heard. It was deafening and, in the awkward boy's mind, it was all about him. The western wrestling fans hated him and hated the Castle family. They were overjoyed that he had lost.

Nick's eyes rolled back as he collapsed to his stomach. He wanted to die. He planted his forehead in the mat, put his hands on the back of his head and wished he could disappear – pondering what else he possibly could have done. The screaming and yelling and roar of the crowd tormented him as he stayed face down and his exhausted opponent rolled off of him.

"What could I have done differently?" he wept. "What more could I have possibly done to prepare? How did I end my high school career without conquering the state tournament to be the best?"

He remained face down, unwilling to look up and acknowledge the world that he lived in … a world with no state title and more, no hope of ever winning one.

* * *

People who have near-death experiences often describe seeing their entire lives pass before their eyes. This was exactly what happened to Nick at that moment as he lay, face down, in front of the crowd, pushing his forehead into the mat.

He saw Ron and himself as elementary school boys wrestling between matches at the Riverside duals and promising themselves and each other that they would be the best ever. He saw Dino and Coach MacCallister believing in him and giving him the focus and confidence to turn around his sophomore season. He saw every practice he had ever gone to and every extra workout he had forced himself to complete ... all in an effort to win a single match ... the match he had just lost.

It seemed like he lay there in front of the packed stadium for hours although, in truth, it was mere moments. He pushed his face into the mat and continued in his despair, even after he heard the voice tell him to "get up."

Chapter 86

GET UP!" the voice repeated. "Be a man. Get up, shake his hand like a man, and get on with your life. He beat you in a fair match. He was the better man tonight, as always. Get to your feet and be a respectful adult."

Nick heeded the voice, only partially realizing that it was emanating from his own mind. It had only been a matter of seconds since the fog horn had sounded but it felt like a week that he had lain, face down in shame, on the wrestling mat. He regained his composure, not because it was what his pride told him to do, but because his conscience said that it was the right thing to do.

Getting up and looking around, all seemed silent. Somehow, the sound of Troftgruben's coach yelling at the referee did not make it to Nick's ears. He was in a daze as he looked around and donned a look of bewilderment as his gaze fell on the scoreboard.

2 – 2, the board read.

"That can't be right," the youth thought. As he looked around, trying to find an explanation, he looked to his corner and found Coach MacCallister who immediately understood his confusion. Nick's coach smiled briefly as he gave Nick the "clasping" sign, and suddenly Nick felt as if he was going to jump through the roof as he hustled back to his corner.

"What's wrong with your foot?" Sean asked.

In his excitement, it hadn't even fully registered with Nick that he was limping.

"I think he landed on my bad ankle in that last flurry," the boy responded.

"Let's tape it up."

A trainer grabbed the medical kit, and MacCallister began taping right over the top of Nick's shoe.

"You asked me earlier," Sean said, "what did I remember most about my time coaching."

Nick got attentive.

"Dino comes to mind," the man continued. "His unquestionable power. Of course, Ron was in there, too, in his recovery after his injury. But ..."

Nick stared at his coach as the man avoided eye contact, focused solely on the tape.

"But what I remember most was a skinny kid – a sophomore with a black eye and a nose full of bloody cotton – getting his butt kicked while wrestling a senior. A wrestler without a chance of winning that night, looked me in the eye and told me, 'I'm not going to lose this match'."

Finishing the taping, MacCallister looked his wrestler in the eye.

"... and then you went out and made it happen."

There was a moment of silence between the two.

"I've always believed in you, Nick," he continued, helping the boy get to his feet. "No matter what happens, that will never change."

Silently, Nick gave Sean a fist-bump and turned back to return to center mat. On the way, the crowd, the ref and the rest of the world faded away. The only thing that remained was the opponent who stood waiting for him.

Chapter 87

To this day, there is no video evidence that shows what happened in overtime. The camera operator who was filming the championship matches to be re-broadcast the following day had not noticed the clasping point and, believing the match to be over, had taken time to verify that he had enough recording capacity for the remaining matches rather than preparing to record the overtime period.

There are different stories of how the match actually ended, but Nick's teammate Seagull swears that it looked painfully brutal as Nick took the first shot, drove off of his injured ankle and grabbed his own crushed fingers in an iron grip. There was a surreal pause as Troftgruben seemed to momentarily hang on defensively before Nick drove with everything he had and took the boy down for two points and the win.

Sean, on the other hand, could not be reached for comment. As Nick finalized his takedown and the ref signaled for two points, the security guard who had caught him earlier showed up at Sean's chair and escorted him from mat-side before Nick even had a chance to say "good bye."

Chapter 88

Nick was beaming until he saw his coach being taken away as he reached down to remove his leg band. The crowd noise was settling down and he glanced up to see his dad in the stands, a few rows above the seats where he expected the man to be. "Was he here all along?" the boy pondered as he glanced up a little further and saw a blonde girl in a lavender coat disappearing through the arena exit.

It was Sandi, he was sure of it. That was her coat.

A mixture of emotions swamped the stoic boy as he went to shake Chester's hand and have his own arm raised.

Chapter 89

Sean followed silently as the security guard led him down a maze of corridors, ranting as they walked.

"Thought you were pretty smart, didn't you? Thought, 'I got away with it once, I'll just push the envelope and get away with it again.' Well, tough luck, mister rebel, you messed with the wrong guy ..."

Sean's mind could not have been further from the droning rambling of the guard's whiny voice and patronizing tone. He thought about Nick winning the state title and weighed that against his own potential legal and career troubles.

"Did you get your kicks on the thrill ride? Was it worth it? ..."

The last sentence did register. Was it worth it? Was helping Nick achieve his dream worth the cost? Would the boy be scarred for life after watching Sean get hauled away in handcuffs by security? He thought back to the goofy, bewildered smile the boy had sported as he finished his high school career, a state champion.

"Yes," he thought. "That answer may change a year from now if I'm living on the streets and getting regular beatings from neighborhood thugs," but, with Nick looking that happy, there was no way that Sean could currently believe that it wasn't worth it.

How unfortunate it was that the same security guard who had seen him earlier at the warm-up mat had noticed him again at mat-side. It almost seemed too convenient, like he had been set up. It was this sentiment that was going through his mind as the guard stopped outside the security office.

Glancing through the window as the guard unlocked the door, Sean's emotions turned from frustration to fury as he saw Mandi and Kreitzer sitting together inside on a couch.

"I was set up," MacCallister thought as his rage peaked. "I'm going to pummel the crap out of him. Why would Mandi help that cretin?"

The guard proudly marched Sean inside and presented him to the head of security, a frazzled-looking man seated at a desk inside the tiny office. Kreitzer just stared at the floor while Mandi looked on with an amused look on her face.

"I caught this rebel rule-breaker ..."

"Where have you been?!!" his superior interrupted him. "You were supposed to be in the main hall by the vendor tables. Some kids stole the cash box from that wrestling author who was autographing books."

"But this guy was ..."

"You were supposed to be in the main hall. We had a robbery and a fight, not to mention these two perverts who I had to pull out of the maintenance closet."

With the last sentence, he motioned to Mandi and Kreitzer.

"But this guy was on the main floor with no credentials coaching one of those kids ..."

"A coach forgot his badge and your thick skull translates that to being more important than the thousands of dollars we're going to get sued for because you weren't doing your job in the main hall?"

Sean watched as Kreitzer finally looked up and, recognizing Sean, got alarmed and climbed to his feet, pointing at MacCallister, "He ..."

"Shut up, idiot!" The supervisor cut Kreitzer off. "You're in enough trouble as it is."

"But I caught ..." the guard tried to make one last pitch before also getting cut off.

"Not another word, Spencer!"

"Did your kid win?" the supervisor asked Sean.

"Yeah," Sean replied with a smile. "Yeah, he did."

"Good. Don't ever lose your credentials again."

Kreitzer again tried to interrupt but was immediately cut off.

"One more time, mister closet, and I'm going to put a muzzle on you. You have the right to remain silent and I suggest that you utilize it until the police get here."

"Spencer, take the coach upstairs, escort him out of the building and get back to your station, NOW!"

Sean cast one final glance at the couch and Mandi made eye contact with a quick wink and a grin. Somehow, he had the feeling he would never see her again to thank her for creating a diversion so that he could coach Nick. He simultaneously felt relief and regret as he was escorted from the room and removed from the building.

He donned his coat and walked toward his Mustang, leaving the capital city knowing that Nick had completed his quest, legal repercussions from Kreitzer were unlikely, and he and Julee had a lot to look forward to in their life together.

Chapter 90

In the dim lights of the civic center, six wrestlers who had weighed in that morning to compete at 152 strode silently to the awards stand. No words were said other than the "Congratulations" and "Good Job" uttered by the athletic director as he gave the boys placing sixth through third their state tournament plaques.

Chester's eyes were vacant as he accepted his award for runner-up, leaving only one competitor remaining to be given a plaque and the state tournament bracket sheet.

The physical world regarded the disheveled Nick Castle as inconsequential among these other wrestlers he had just bested. Yet, it isn't the physical world that determines a person's value or their place in history. For all intents and purposes, the top step could have been left empty. The desire, tenacity and fight were not tangible but were what had enabled the boy to get to the top spot.

As the state's "Mr. Wrestling" accepted his plaque for the 152-pound state championship with a broad grin crossing his face, the athletic director commented on how Nick had not only won the state championship, but had also beaten the 145- and 160-pound champions over the course of the season. Watching without blinking, Daunte Broadsetter and hundreds of other kids in the audience felt that they, too, could one day ascend to the top of the podium.

Amid the cheering, Daunte pulled on his father's shirtsleeve again and whispered, "Dad, I'm going to be like that boy..."

Then, he turned to watch again as the wrestlers stood tall and continued, "... some day, I'm going to be the best."

Epilogue

Sean departed the Castle farmstead as the snow continued to fall. A mile later, he rolled the Mustang to a stop, reached for the envelope in the passenger seat and engaged the dome light.

Sitting at the side of the road with the storm swirling outside reminded him of several years earlier when his Galaxie 500 had given out. Ted Graham's words from that same day flashed through Sean's mind.

"If you're going to die in a tragic way, I suppose falling asleep in the cold is the least painful way to go. You just don't wake up."

In the past year Sean had lost everything in his life he cherished. It had started with his sister Amy and her family moving to Europe with the military. Soon after that came Julee's accident and coma. Sean had spent most waking hours at her side, using up all of his vacation and personal time at work and having to take many unpaid days to be with her. In the prior years, after getting married, the two had been prudent in paying off their debt and managed to even save a bit for retirement. With the expense of her constant care, they had lost all of that and became buried in medical bills, much deeper in debt than Sean had ever been before.

Having lost his nest egg, Sean soon also left his job. Growing Roadrunner to a shining star had been his closest experience to raising a child. Internal politics aside, he loved those he had worked with and didn't want to burden them missing more days of work. Moving Julee to a facility closer to her parents gave him partners to share his vigil, but his job search in the new city had dragged on for over three months. Sean moved into the cheapest apartment he could find and sold all of their belongings except the fully restored Mustang, which he needed for sentimental reasons and transportation.

Watching her lie there so peacefully made him remember how upbeat Julee had been, years ago telling him, "Our physical bodies eventually give out but I'm going to stay happy while I'm here and take that into the next world."

When the doctors told him her condition was permanent, Sean succumbed to despair. He struggled for reasons to continue on and wondered, should he completely fold, whether or not his emotional torment would accompany him into the afterworld. It was the day before Thanksgiving after he left her hospital room that he reached the end of his rope and convinced himself that Kelly was the only one who could possibly help him through. He ventured out into the storm, hit the city limits and kept going.

Now, twelve hours later, he sat in the Mustang and used his pocket knife to open up Nick's envelope. Inside was the picture of Sean and Nick that Mrs. Castle had taken after the Capital tournament Nick's junior year. They both looked so young – half the age that Sean could remember feeling in any recent year.

The young man grinned, thinking back to that match which had both followed and preceded some tumultuous times. He turned the picture over and found a handwritten note from Nick, written that same season.

> Coach,
>> Thank you for believing in me and always being there for me. You made me the wrestler and the person I am today.
>> Nick

Sean sat in silence. With no family, no job, no prospects and no direction, his life seemed relatively hopeless. Yet his impact on at least one other life was now abundantly clear. It was time to focus on the things that he did have – a slim possibility of Julee recovering, a functioning Mustang, half a tank of gas, a new suit, and the potential to change lives.

He clicked off the dome light, put the car in gear, and ventured out to find the next phase of his life.

* * *

Nick had watched as the Mustang made its way down the long dirt driveway of the Castle farmstead. He had waved one final time as the car stopped briefly and signaled before turning onto the county road and disappearing into the snow and darkness of the stormy night.

"Coach MacCallister," he thought, wondering whether or not his coach had opened the envelope. "It was nice to have known you."

As with all mentor relationships, there comes a time when the mentee needs to move on and find his own way. As Nick headed back into his family house, his mind was filled with memories of the years he and his coach had just re-lived. Through the ups and downs of life, he was thankful for all of the people who had made the journey with him and helped him to develop into the young man he had become.

Yet, it gave him pause as he pondered who it was he had become and exactly what next steps might be for him. He went to the family room and glanced out the window at the darkness and swirling snow. What had he really become and where was he going?

This was the first year in well over a decade that he had not wrestled. Failure to beat-out Chester for a spot on the university roster and nagging injuries convinced him that it was time to focus on his studies and dedicate his time to preparing for his career. Yet, tonight it seemed that there should be a way to give back to the sport that had consumed so much of his life. Perhaps he should look into coaching a junior high team or maybe even getting a job as an assistant coach for the Riverside / South program. Some of the wrestlers he had coached years ago were getting to their early high school years. Could he do justice to coaching them while still focusing on his own schoolwork? Could he be the kind of coach that MacCallister and Nestor had been to him?

In high school, things had seemed so straightforward. He was going to win the state championship and the rest of life was going to take care of itself. But that was so long ago and there was so much life to still be lived. While he didn't know how much of his life he would be able to control, he did know that he needed to start by finishing college to give himself a strong base. Of course, that would mean passing his literature class, which he had found a way to avoid for so many years. His brain was better suited for math and accounting, but tonight he promised himself that he would work on his writing assignment and get himself one step closer to a college degree. He had the entire Thanksgiving weekend to focus on his project. Maybe he would surprise himself and write something that people would want to read. Of course if that happened, he'd have to pick a pen name so that people couldn't find him and make him go on TV or speak in public. Maybe he could follow in the steps of S.E. Hinton or J.K. Rowling.

Stopping at the fireplace, he looked on the mantle and saw his and Ron's state championship plaques, still proudly adorned there years later. "That was a goal worth pursuing," he thought as a smile crossed his lips. His mind drifted back to the ceremony at which his name was unveiled, carved into the ring of honor in the Riverside wrestling room. Principal Skinner had called him a week after he had won the state championship and had asked for permission to add Nick's name to the ring.

"You're the only wrestler to ever compete for Riverside who has been named Mr. Wrestling for the state," the man had commented. "With the Riverside and South programs combining next year, we would like to carve your name into the wall with our other wrestling greats."

As honored as Nick had been, he did take the time to negotiate one detail in that he wanted his name to be placed between Ron's and Dino's. Two years of consternation about Dino's name being excluded was soon rectified as Skinner was persuaded by Coach Nestor that, since several South wrestlers who had barely missed receiving state titles had been included on the school's wrestling plaque, Dino's name certainly belonged on the wall.

Tanner and Patron had been at the ceremony. For the next few years, the three had remained close until Tanner graduated and moved away for college and Patron found a girlfriend who convinced him to move out-of-state.

Nick felt the familiar nudge of a dog's nose against his hand and bent down to give Chewie a kiss on the snout.

"There's my good boy," he told the aged animal who could no longer run as his accident and the subsequent onset of arthritis held him back. Yet, the value of a dog is far less physical than emotional. As Sandi had stated, he was a big furry lump of love sent from God and Nick appreciated him for what he was.

"Sandi," Nick thought. He had heard from her a few days earlier. She was coming home from France for Christmas break and wanted to see him. It had made Nick's girlfriend furious that he still kept in touch with Sandi but, realistically, that relationship wasn't headed in the right direction anyway. Maybe he and Sandi just needed to wait for the right time to end up together.

"Enough stalling," he thought. "Write something down so that you don't fail this darn class."

But what? With everything milling around in his head, he eventually came up with a first line.

"The two wrestlers faced each other; neither blinked. This was the championship match. While both boys felt unbeatable, only one would prove himself to be so tonight."

He stopped for a moment and looked at the words. He was pretty sure that anything that started out that way would earn him a B at best, yet as his thoughts gelled, he realized that he had a lot more to write. With his dog at his side, he continued writing well into the night.